Praise for Javier Serena's *Last Words on Earth*

"This is a wonder."—*Publishers Weekly* (Starred Review)

"More than a novel about Roberto Bolaño, *Last Words on Earth* is a story about passion, sacrifice, and the uncompromising pursuit of literature. Not simply for fans of the writer, but anyone touched by the power of books and writing."—Mark Haber, author of *Lesser Ruins*

"*Last Words on Earth* is a good novel. It works. It's a kind of fan fiction, though perhaps we won't call it that because fan fiction is low class, and Bolaño is high and literary (and instead of recycling the author's characters, it's the author himself who is raised from the dead and reanimated). But like fan fiction, it works because it *satisfies*, because it answers questions that otherwise go unanswered in the holes and omissions (and final foreclosure) of Bolaño's life story."—Aaron Bady, *Los Angeles Review of Books*

"Serena channels his observations about creativity into elegant sentences (via Whittemore's translation) that evoke the storm-clouded intensity of Bolaño's prose in books like *2666*."—*Kirkus Reviews*

"Serena writes fluidly and well—and manages a Bolañoesque feel not only to the character but also to his voice [. . .] a good and well-told story."—Michael Orthofer, *Complete Review*

Also in English Translation by Javier Serena

Last Words on Earth

ATTILA

Javier Serena

Translated from Spanish by Katie Whittemore

Originally published in Spanish as *Atila. Un eseritor indescifrable* by Tropo Editores, 2014

Copyright © Javier Serena, 2014

Translation copyright © Katie Whittemore, 2025

This edition is published by arrangement with International Editors' Co.

First edition, 2025

All rights reserved

Library of Congress Control Number: 2024952583

ISBN (pb): 978-1-960385-35-2| ISBN (ebook): 978-1-960385-36-9

This project is made possible by the New York State Council on the Arts with the support of the Office of the Governor and the New York State Legislature.

Cover design by Daniel Benneworth-Gray

Published by Open Letter at the University of Rochester

Morey Hall 303, Rochester NY, 14627

www.openletterbooks.org

Printed on acid-free paper.

ATTILA

I

HE ALWAYS RESPONDED in the most eccentric possible way: and so on finding himself alone and confused, ostracized and adrift in Paris, instead of giving up, Alioscha chose to entrench himself even deeper in his writing obsession. I confirmed this for myself mere hours after landing in Paris. Uneasy about his state of mind and fearing he'd gone mad following the desertion of his latest female companion, I searched for him everywhere, seeking any sign that he was still alive, finally locating him in the expanses of the Parc de Belleville. It was a serendipitous discovery. I'd gone to that place with its exceptional panoramic views on a whim, trying to kill time, resigned that I'd have to wait until the next day to try and talk to him, but upon reaching a cluster of graffitied wooden benches at the top of the hill and looking to my right, I suddenly found myself confronted by my friend's solemn and tragic silhouette, set against the Parisian rooftops. The figure he cut revealed that, over the past few weeks, he'd only sunk deeper into the delirious swamp in which he already flailed. He looked like a soloist seized by a musical fever, moving his lips to a melody only he could hear, his hair whipped about by the wind and his body in the throes of a strange vibration, so abstracted and brooding that he seemed entirely indifferent to his surroundings, wholly focused on reading from a piece of paper held inches from his face. Only when I got closer, when I could finally hear the absurd litany he was muttering, hand clenched in a claw, did I realize without surprise that I was witnessing a kind of theatrical rehearsal in that secluded spot: Alioscha slowly and deliberately reciting the most recent chapter of Attila, the novel he'd been writing for years and whose long and chaotic discourse of impossible verses and nonsensical paragraphs he would finish just days before he killed himself.

But it would take until October for Alioscha to finish his book, and at that time it was only February, a raw winter afternoon on which Alioscha seemed immune to the cold and the vast and naked sky, so absorbed in his words that he remained completely unaware of my presence until I tapped him on the shoulder.

He turned, startled, as disoriented as if he'd just surfaced from the ocean's depths. But when he saw it was me, he smiled and embraced me warmly, remembering out loud that I had, just one week prior, in fact, advised him of the time and date of my arrival.

"I thought it was Tuesday, that tomorrow was Wednesday!" he said, pained by his mistake. "Otherwise I wouldn't have left the house until you got in!"

He rambled on, apologizing for his confusion until he appeared to accept that there was nothing to be done about the mix-up and instead began to tell me about the progress on his book.

"I finished another chapter yesterday," he said, holding up the pages, purposefully avoiding any discussion of the details surrounding his new life situation. "In a few months, I'll have written the last page."

This seemed to be his only aim: to finish the book as soon as possible, working around the clock, refusing to feel sorry for himself over Camille's jilting, taking refuge in his idiosyncratic endeavor to string together words and thereby not confront the absolute isolation in which he was immersed. He clearly avoided the subject of his reclusion as we looked for the exit from the park, for as we climbed stairs and left ponds and leaf-strewn dirt paths behind us, Alioscha wanted only to talk about his recent reading and certain technical aspects of his book, making no mention of the despair I knew the young university student must have caused him. Nor did he confide in me when, having left the bounds of the park, we ran out of literary topics to discuss. As we moved farther from where I had found him, I remained uncertain whether Camille's departure was a temporary, mutual decision, or if she had unilaterally resolved never to sleep in my friend's company again. Regardless of what Alioscha did or did not tell me, he certainly showed obvious signs of having gone too long with no one to talk to: it was partly the nervous way he had of speaking, his expressions more clipped and abundant than usual, along with the worsening of his physical appearance, evidenced by long greasy hair and obvious pallor.

And yet, I actually found him to be in much better shape than I'd imagined a week before, when my home phone in Madrid rang in the wee hours of the morning. Alarmed by the untimely noise, I grabbed the receiver and heard the voice of a sick and dying man, a voice slow and thick, as if he'd been drinking alone, and which disclosed—with no apology for waking me—that Camille had left him. "Now I don't have to worry about keeping tabs on her temperature or the violent coughing fits," he mumbled ironically. "Now I can spend hours and hours writing with no other obligation except to remember to breathe." That night he spoke in a passionless monotone, muted by somnolence, and before he hung up to drown in his own darkness, I lied and told him I already had a ticket to Paris for the following week. And I wasn't the only one alarmed by the fateful bit of news that Alioscha had lost the young student's companionship. When I relayed the news to him the next morning—as we were wont to do in such situations—his cousin Carlos Valls replied with a fateful prediction, a deep truth, the truest and most chilling, and one neither of us wanted to accept: "It could be now or in a few years," he sighed, making his dark prophecy, "but one of these days Alioscha's going to jump in the Seine with an anvil around his neck."

It was his only plausible end. And yet, though Alioscha had always harbored an intense suicidal calling—over the years we could all see how he walked, unflinching, toward the brink of death—it was also true that when I set off on my rescue mission to Paris, it still seemed too soon for that fate, given that my friend was so consumed by writing that he hadn't the time to think about hanging himself.

Such was the state affairs that early evening as we walked aimlessly in the vicinity of his neighborhood, Alioscha again insisting on the classical resonances in his novel, which he declared was structured around the patterns in specific Greek myths, and then making an offhand mention of his nonessential job at a nursing home in the Saint-Denis district. "It's still just Saturdays and Sundays, and they're not completely off their rocker," he said with a complicit smile, reminding me of the afternoon I visited the home and caught him organizing a sort of clandestine sock-hop. "I bring the manuscript with me and start revising the second I get on the bus."

He moved frenetically as we walked, animated, possessed by his typically fantastical nature, which had always allowed him to remain outside the coercive norms of constraint and decorum and often led to scenes that illustrated the extravagant character that had governed Alioscha since the day he was born. For instance, when we passed a few garbage bins on the street near the market and discovered, to our surprise, a pile of discarded books on the ground between them, Alioscha couldn't resist such tempting rubbish and stopped to ransack them with gusto, throwing popular novels over his shoulder and rescuing a few volumes missing their covers. Shortly thereafter, having ticked off a list of important writers who had disavowed their home countries, he pulled me along on another irrepressible impulse to an alley near his apartment, a passageway littered with cigarette butts and broken bottles, where he showed me a plaque menaced by rust and inscribed with a short mention of the English poet who died there nearly a century before. But the moment that sparked his heartiest enthusiasm wasn't when he came across a few decent books, dozens of copies of which could be found in the Paris kiosks, nor when he stood before the house of that nineteenth-century writer whose name I'd never heard, but when he suggested we visit a pond so small it was practically hidden, where we could feed red fish stale bread. No time for explanations, no answers to my questions, taking hold of my jacket so I wouldn't slow us down at traffic lights, Alioscha rushed me to a secluded square with a small pool of dirty water, where he pulled a crust of bread from his pocket and began sprinkling crumbs here and there, trying to stir up the fish. Before we left, he stuck his hand in the water so they could feed greedily from the palm of his hand.

But the sight of him so joyous, so exuberant over his juvenile exploits, did not afford me the sense of peace I might've expected. In fact, it frightened me. And no wonder. I knew well that the lonelier and more desperate Alioscha became, the more compulsive about his work, the more sudden and intense his waves of irrational optimism, the deeper the resulting void that followed. Only when night fell and winter's early shadows grew sharp and dense and a dry wind froze the streets, only when Alioscha caught a bit of a melody coming from a nearby shop and was suddenly overcome by a fit of nostalgia and all his anguish rushed to the fore, only then did he make a moving admission about his short, tortured romance with Camille. After a thoughtful silence, he stopped and wearily observed the pavement. Shoulders hunched and hands deep in the pockets of his trench coat, Alioscha confessed that he spent restless nights embracing a pillow, clinging to the illusion that he was holding a woman's soft body, and other, even worse nights when he woke from the sinister nightmare that Camille had returned, only to desert him again. "And it's not just my subconscious betraying me," he said. "I call for her when I'm awake, too, even though I know she'll never come, like it's enough just to hear my own voice."

After that, everything he said and did revolved around his memories of Camille. With a dejected gait, ignoring his untied shoelaces and the drivers that honked when he blindly stepped into the road, numb to everything but thoughts of the young student, he pulled me over to a bench by the Seine where he claimed to have seen her for the first time, and then on to a centuries-old tree famous for its height, where he swore that, in a teenage impulse, he'd carved his name and hers into the trunk with a knife. Then, evoking their early days—the only easy and happy time they'd shared—his tour took us to the home of Camille's aunt, and there under the balcony he muttered and cursed the paradoxes of love, convinced that his happiest days with the girl had been at the beginning, when she still lived under her family's roof and he'd delighted in running around half the city on foot just to see her for a few minutes.

But the most eloquent signs of his grief, those which mercilessly showed all he lacked, arose when we stopped in front of the main building of the Sorbonne, a place that was for him steeped in both sentiment and scars, and where, with a mix of guilt and sorrow, he recalled that when he'd met her, Camille had been an exceptional student.

"She always went to class. Everyday. Even when she had a fever," he said in the middle of the cobblestone square, thinking of the times he'd waited for her, tucked away in some corner. He would start watching the door well before eight o'clock, and she would rush out to him the moment her class was over, mindful she wasn't being followed.

And though he spoke as if describing scenes from a distant past, his recollection of those early meetings convinced Alioscha that he had to find out right then and there whether or not she had resumed her studies. We approached this undertaking with all the necessary precautions, sidestepping the main stairs, aware that—if she discovered us—Camille would likely be furious and set to beating my friend about the head with her purse. And so, having discarded a plan to hide among the columns at the entrance, we finally sheltered in a doorway dimly lit by a flickering streetlight that only revealed us intermittently, located at one end of the square where students and residents passed by, more concerned with their conversations than what was happening in the street. But despite our vigilance, we never saw her among the groups of students when the day's last classes let out, nor with the professors who lagged behind, nor when almost all the lights were switched off and only a few increasingly ambiguous shapes remained visible inside the building. But instead of leaving, instead of taking refuge from the freezing night air in some bar, we lingered in the shadows until past eight o'clock, quiet and expectant, Alioscha glancing about and me trying to look inconspicuous, less motivated now by the hope of hearing Camille's quick footsteps and more by the desire to pay homage to the ghosts of the past. We didn't even make to leave when the last bells of a nearby church tolled, and no one was left in the square except a dog and his owner. We only moved off when Alioscha grew tired, so late by then that only the night watchmen remained, and we did so very slowly and in silence, each pained by our own dark angst, each longing, perhaps, for some vague homeland existing only in the purest fantasy, each with the same bitter and futureless melancholy of a pair of men who had spent many years in exile.

ALIOSCHA ONLY REVEALED the details surrounding Camille's desertion the next morning, in the middle of the crowded Belleville market—one of Paris's noisiest spots—at a stall consisting of a tarp covering three long tables heaped with bags and wallets and other poor-quality leather goods. It was an off-the-cuff confession. We had been strolling the market from end to end, not paying particular attention to any vendor, impervious to the fabrics and fruit-filled baskets on offer, when we passed a narrow side aisle and Alioscha, having spotted some studded belts, stopped to examine them.

He rifled indifferently through the merchandise, as if already familiar with the stock, and then, after a prolonged silence, spoke Camille's name.

"One day she woke up with the highest temperature she'd had in weeks, soaked in cold sweat," Alioscha said, picking up and discarding handbags and wallets at random, so abstracted that he seemed to be muttering to himself. "She realized she couldn't go on much longer like that."

It was the explanation I hadn't dared to ask him for. Avoiding my eyes, Alioscha recounted how at the end of December,

Camille had suffered from high fevers that left her vomiting through the night. Even so, he persisted in trying to cure her by his own methods, afraid he would lose her if he took her to a hospital. But, he went on to admit, despite the fact that he went broke buying ineffectual drugs and searched his medical school textbooks for alternative therapies, not only did he fail to restore her to health, but her condition worsened. This went on until one morning when Camille was forced to admit her mistake, and forgetting the promises she made in the euphoria of her flight from her family home, demanded to speak to her parents. In his recollection of those hours, Alioscha, who had always catered to her every whim, said that he brought the phone to the bed willingly, though he knew that once Camille contacted her father, the man would come immediately to take her away.

"She poured it all out she the minute the phone was in her hand, confessed everything she'd been hiding for eight months: where she lived and with whom and how much she regretted having gone missing for so long," continued Alioscha, who claimed he'd had to lean against the wall for support as he listened in. "She cried and asked them to come and get her as soon as they could, swearing up and down that she would never do anything so stupid again."

Based on what I gathered from Alioscha's story, Camille's father, terrified by his daughter's confession, made a frantic trip to Paris from Tours and turned up at Alioscha's basement apartment that very night, as furious as if he really had been rescuing the young student from a kidnapper. The man's reaction was easy to imagine: horror when faced with the squalor of the musty and unventilated apartment, and rage at finding his daughter prostrate on a mattress as decrepit as an old cot in a war hospital.

"I showed him which medications I'd been giving her," he brooded as the handbag vendor eyed him with growing suspicion. "But there was no way to calm him down: he was livid, like he couldn't even believe that we'd been living in such a hole—he kept repeating that it looked like a broom closet, or catacombs."

What most affected Alioscha, however, wasn't the father's rancor, which he must have expected, but that the man who hated him for having taken away his daughter should ultimately show him pity. Witnessing firsthand Alioscha's preposterous state of poverty, the man realized that he was nothing but a poor wretch blinded by his own naive Romantic illusions. And seeing him so helpless, so alone and unbalanced in the chaos of the apartment glutted with books and smudged papers, Camille's father took his leave with the same gesture of compassion he would have shown a pauper.

"He opened his wallet and gave me all the money he had on him," Alioscha said, looking at me at last as he moved away from the stall, which we'd been blocking for several minutes without making a purchase. "And before he left with Camille, he gave me a card with his address and phone number and asked if I had any family that could help."

He wouldn't provide any more detail, not even whether he'd been able say goodbye to Camille, though as we left the market, I had the impression that he was always thinking of the girl and the futility of winning her back. Alioscha understandably feared the definitive nature of such farewells: after all, just two years before, in a foreshadowing of the spiral of loneliness in which he would sink ever deeper, Élene—his wife and only ally since the day he left Barcelona—had up and abandoned him in the wee hours of the morning, tired of the anachronistic tics of a failed writer who had moved them to Paris.

In truth, anything I knew about Alioscha's history with Élene I'd learned from Carlos Valls, my main confidant, given that she had already left their apartment in Oberkampf for good by the time I first met Alioscha. So it was only thanks to the recollections of his cousin—as intrigued as I by the mystery of the man who had been his closest companion since childhood—that I heard how Alioscha and Élene had settled in Paris, enchanted by what Alioscha saw as the city's mythical aura, which lasted until the third or fourth year when Élene began to sense the cracks that threatened her husband's fantasies in which he'd become a respected novelist and she a great avant-garde painter. Carlos Valls had seemed certain that the couple's relationship couldn't have ended any other way. He remarked how, with Alioscha so absorbed in his writing, it was only logical that Élene—a discreet, balanced, and quiet woman—would feel increasingly defrauded, ever farther from her original goal, and would eventually come to the conclusion that the best thing was for her to open their front door and vanish, aware that if she kept living with Alioscha, she'd only become more lost in his asphyxiating labyrinth.

In any case, I gleaned that his relationship with Camille had been different in every sense, given that it had been short-lived, and there hadn't been the same intermittent periods of harmony. Yet, as with his wife, their relationship had come to the same irrecoverable end. The affair had been shorter, much shorter, hardly eight months, and its conclusion, therefore, couldn't be attributed to the eventual tedium inherent to cohabitation, to the shadows and silences that had gradually tarnished his life with Élene, but rather to an original misalignment, an older and more insurmountable breach far exceeding simple boredom, given that they'd been submerged in a state of deep and permanent tension ever since they'd moved to the basement rooms in Belleville. It quickly became clear that they had both fallen prey to a fleeting mirage they never should have indulged in. She was a beautiful young woman, unpredictable and capricious, who had only recently arrived in the city with a desire to lose herself in the Parisian night and its shadowy recesses, while Alioscha was already a grown man who behaved with monastic discipline, uninterested in parties and engrossed in his writerly routines. And to make matters worse, they'd known each other such a short time and so superficially that Camille's disenchantment arrived almost simultaneous to the moment she began to share his bed, making him feel guilty for ever having courted her and convinced her to leave her aunt's house. Over the course of their months together, both Carlos Valls and I were witness to Camille's continual displays of anger. More than once we saw her interrupt Alioscha while he was speaking, cutting him off mid-sentence, or ignoring him when he asked her a question, or berating him for having bought cheaper soap than she was used to or because the milk he put in her coffee was too hot and burned her tongue.

It was an untenable situation, a painful and degrading reality no good for either one of them. Yet Camille resisted the relationship's failure out of pure obstinacy, forcing herself to endure the mistake that originated on the night she called her father and told him she was starting her adventure as an emancipated woman. She hid behind her declaration of self-sufficiency for months, anxious, beside herself, trapped by her lies and her pride, too stubborn to admit her mistake, until the end of December when she fell gravely ill and had to choose between accepting defeat or dying in the company of a démodé troubadour.

She chose to live, and so abandoned Alioscha, who was left alone and one step away from madness or death.

He still maintained that, with time, he would have cured her, and that the success of his books was imminent, which was why he claimed to have the terrible sense of having been the victim of some misunderstanding. That might have explained some of his behavior, like how he returned to the Sorbonne day after day in the weeks following Camille's departure, still rattled by the young woman's disappearance, unable to accept that she'd gotten fed up with spending her nights shivering with cold.

My friend's despondence caused me to make that visit to Paris my longest in the city, partly because I was worried and partly in solidarity, given the neglected state in which he'd been left. I stayed for almost two weeks, not enough time to see him recover, true, but sufficient to ascertain that Camille had indeed been his last chance at salvation: he subjected himself to such a peculiar lifestyle that he would never find another person who was willing to sleep in his bed. Besides, his economic insecurity was by then fully apparent. He lived off his paltry savings, what remained of a family inheritance, and the money he earned working in the nursing home. His income was so minimal that he'd turned to collecting bags of trash from his neighbors in the noisy building where he lived, in exchange for them covering his water and electricity, a new role that obliged him to cut his activities short at ten p.m. on the dot. Because of this responsibility, if the appointed time drew near while we chatted on the paths in the Parc de Belleville or some other remote part of the city, he would ask that we quickly make our way back to his building, where he would then go door to door hauling the bags his neighbors left out for him. Alioscha didn't seem to be frustrated by his circumstances. Quite the opposite: he accepted them with punctual docility, attentive and conscientious, as if he didn't notice the humiliation inherent to the task, impervious to the jokes and laughter, and so used to coping with failure that he wasn't even rattled when they mocked him by setting out bags filled with rocks.

Yet what did still pain Alioscha deeply was the hushed memory of Camille, to which he continued to pay homage with incomprehensible ceremonies celebrated to appease his fantasy, such as the melancholy custom of showing up at the university gates with the quite unreasonable hope that she had resumed her studies instead of returning to Tours. Stranger yet was how he continued to set a place for her at the table, as if they were about to share a meal, or continuing to sleep on the couch so that the bed remained available for Camille's feverish body. And those were just the more routine practices, which at times seemed designed to invoke her and others to simply stave off boredom: he'd also discovered new rituals, darker and more somber, like the way he disposed of the clothes she'd left behind, a process that seemed to be guided by a peculiar, sentimental intuition. Once, in the wee hours of the morning, I watched him lug a suitcase stuffed with shirts and sweaters to a church doorstep. Another day, I caught him filling a sack with several pairs of her shoes, which he later strung up from a solitary tree. And one overcast afternoon, I was witness to how he tossed a bag containing several pieces of her lingerie into the Seine, sighing all the while.

And yet it wasn't all laments with him, since—as was often the case—the sadder and more alone he felt, the worse his ostracism in Paris, the more any ordinary event could enchant him. His faithful visits to the pond to feed the red fish, for instance, or his juvenile penchant for stealing from secondhand bookshops. And along with those more mundane pastimes, which I'd seen him enjoy for years, another more exciting and surprising hobby emerged: taking photographs on the street and developing the film in his apartment using a slow artisanal process.

He claimed it was a sudden passion, born by coincidence: one day he was rummaging around in the nursing home attic, through the cast-off chairs and chipped lamps, exploring the contents of the same trunk from which he'd rescued a busted radio and an old record player, and discovered a camera. His dismal economic circumstances meant he'd had to learn the secrets of the photographer's art on his own. He developed the film himself, in the shower, following a meticulous and burdensome operation that he nonetheless seemed to enjoy, engrossed in the languid labor of transformation, as delighted as if it were alchemical magic. Afterward, when the process was complete and the images had been rescued from the nebula of the film roll, he stacked them on his writing desk, or laid them out on the couch, or left them hung up with clothespins on the drying line for a few days. But what my friend liked most was the thrill of shooting in the streets. That visit, whenever we met for a walk, Alioscha turned up with the camera around his neck, as if it were a part of his antiquated outfit, the most valuable and important accessory, the most extraordinary: the only thing that allowed him to momentarily suspend his nostalgia for Camille. He had fixed obsessions. He usually photographed people, not landscapes, and almost always opted for a woman's face, whether it was a radiant girl waiting at a stoplight, or a woman reflected for a blurry instant in the top half of a mirror. He never had a plan. He worked as if guided by amazement, fascinated by a unique set of features or smile, drawn to some deliberate gesture, a businesswoman's elegant gait. They were impulsive acts, maneuvers in which Alioscha lurched abruptly, hunched over, running or climbing a fence or pressing himself to a storefront window, oblivious to the effect he was having on his model. He looked happy as we walked, pleased to be carrying a piece of the city inside his camera, jubilant over the ecstasy of the hunt. That is, until sundown, when the time came for us to say goodnight and Alioscha stumbled again over his shattered reality. His transformation was notable. Crestfallen and grave, he made plans for us to meet for lunch the next day, then walked slowly away down the sidewalk, eyes lowered and shoulders slumped. He never looked back and was always much sadder than at the beginning the day, as if wrapped in a funeral shroud, aware that the only signs of life awaiting him in his basement rooms were the portraits he'd hung there to dry.

So passed several of the days during which I witnessed firsthand the angst affecting Alioscha, a pain old and deep that followed him like a curse through the anonymity of Paris. In truth, I couldn't do much in our short time together besides confirm his grim condition as an exile—even though that term wasn't entirely accurate in his case. By unspoken agreement, we organized our days much like we had on my previous visits: I would spend the early part of the morning by myself, working on my articles and features, while he immersed himself in writing his novel of indecipherable paragraphs. Then around one o'clock, by which time Alioscha had used up all the strength he'd managed to store during his fitful nights, we would meet for lunch in some Belleville restaurant near his apartment, then stroll with no fixed destination, long walks that sometimes stretched on under the lit streetlamps, depending on the urgency he felt to get back to his desk. Now that he was on his own and with no one to talk to, a ghost stranded in a village of ghosts, he sometimes preferred to leave his writing for later and prolong our time together so that he could leisurely digress on his incurable abstractions.

Alioscha and I always ended our evenings before the ten p.m. trash collection, so I never did see him up to his neck in that disreputable muck, soiled by mockery and scorn, filth and fruit peels, until the very last night of my visit when, thanks to an oversight, I returned to his apartment after we'd already said goodnight.

The origin of the mix-up could be traced back to that day's lunch, when we got up to leave after coffee and dessert and Alioscha—distracted by his despair over Camille—left the little bag of bread he'd saved for the fish on the table. I put the bag in my pocket and promptly forgot it myself until a few minutes before ten o'clock, as I strolled alone down a poorly lit avenue, my mind far from Paris, preoccupied with getting back to the hotel and packing for my flight. Stepping onto the curb to hail a passing taxi, I put my hand in my coat pocket and felt the little bundle of bread from lunch. All I wanted was to rest, to take refuge from the intense chill of the February wind, but I remembered how Alioscha insisted that his beloved fish had adapted their feeding schedule to his visits. Certain that my friend's ritual of sprinkling crumbs on the dirty pond was important, I apologized to the driver in the waiting taxi and found myself making the trip on foot back to Alioscha's basement apartment. I was distracted and subdued, thinking of the assignments awaiting me in Madrid, and didn't consider the fact that my friend would, at that very moment, be engaged in the thankless task of collecting the neighbors' trash. I wasn't thinking of it as I made my way down the gloomy street toward his lair, just like I hadn't given it much thought on any other day, all the times he bid me goodnight, forever in a rush, at the mercy of the strict punctuality of the municipal garbage truck.

It only occurred to me when I neared his building and was forced to remember, for just as I was about to cross the street, I saw a group of teenagers heckling Alioscha as he grappled with the trash bags. I stopped on the darkened corner and waited in stillness. A streetlamp was angled over the scene before me, a weak stage light accentuating the impoverished set Alioscha seemed to have built for himself: Belleville itself was a busy, central neighborhood, but his building stood on a side street with worse lighting than its neighbors, as if he created his own outskirts wherever he called home.

Realizing that the drudge work of dealing with the entire building's refuse also came with a daily dose of humiliation and contempt, I stood quietly for a few more moments, unsure whether or not I should cross the street, feeling my friend's suffering but aware there was nothing I could do to help him: the kids' jeers and bold stares left no room for doubt. As Alioscha was depositing a load of bags into the bins, one of his aggressors spoke from his perch on the fence and the others exploded in loud laughter. My friend ignored the provocation, focused on his job, immune to their insults, resigned to handling the garbage with striking passivity. Still unaware of my presence, his eyes fixed on the ground, Alioscha went back inside with an automaton's steady march, quick and methodical, and in the streetlamp's fragile light, his face contained a new expression, a deadened grimace reminiscent of the tortured figures held aloft on the shoulders of religious penitents in procession.

Alioscha returned with more bags every few minutes, the time it took for him to go upstairs and come down with another load, indifferent to his surroundings, imperturbable in spite of the grime and carnivalesque atmosphere that accompanied every round. He looked serious, very serious, like a condemned man appearing before the crowd, his face tight and sallow, the same sickly appearance as if he'd been locked away in a forgotten dungeon. But it was his composure that made the sad situation even sadder. He carried on as if nothing were wrong while the young men accosted him, deaf to their jeers, refusing to look at them or respond in any way, his sole concern to finish the job on time, operating with a speed and punctiliousness that cast him as even more pathetic and amusing to his audience. How could he tolerate such a situation? Perhaps he accepted such disgrace as part of his writerly legend, or maybe it was simply a quick and easy way to save money while he endeavored to write *Attila*. Whatever his calculus, I watched from the opposite sidewalk as he remained stoic, even when they threw a cigarette butt at his turned back or plopped a banana peel on his shoulder or amused themselves by moving the bins farther down the street. Unmoved by their provocations, Alioscha labored on, assured that the battle he was sworn to fight was not to be waged on Belleville sidewalks, but on the pages he wrote.

The sight I found most distressing, the vision that kept me from going over and giving him his fish food, was the mishap that occurred once the garbage truck had appeared at the end of the street, headlights submerged in the night like a ship entering an inhospitable port on the Brittany coast. The accident unfolded in a matter of seconds, when the truck was already stopped in front of the building next door, ready to lift and empty the dumpsters, and Alioscha was running down with the last of the bags. The kid on the fence, the first one to taunt him, shoved one of his companions, who in turn fell into my friend, who had no one else to stop him, and in the chaos of stumbling, tumbling bodies, it was Alioscha who ended up on the ground awash in crumpled wrappers and food scraps. He didn't react. Uncomplaining, barely looking up to confirm that the truck was still idling, Alioscha stooped to pick up the scattered debris, ignoring the commotion around him, careful not to leave behind any pieces of paper or fruit peels, attempting to scuff the coffee grounds and cigarette ash off the pavement with his shoe.

With a squeal of brakes and grinding of the clutch, the truck shifted into gear, coming to an almost immediate stop outside Alioscha's building, its bright headlights illuminating all the ugliness. Alioscha redoubled his efforts so as not to slow the usual pace of the collection, while a half dozen of his neighbors cheered his new show of submission. It was too much for me. Alarmed by the knowledge that such hell was routine, convinced that I could do nothing but witness his torment, I decided to leave before he'd finished, and as I moved off in search of a taxi back to my hotel, I thought about how much Alioscha must have had to suffer before being able to remain unaffected by those insults, and how unfair it was that such a thing was happening to someone like him, a person whose only sin was to bravely defend the one thing he believed in.

That image, his acceptance of defeat, his scrabbling about in the midst of ridicule, his vulnerability, was a good illustration of what had always been his destiny, the fate of one who chose to be consumed by a single idea. And the more courageous and sincere his commitment, the more he suffered, and the more he suffered, the stronger he persisted in his attempt, as if instead of being a writer whose books nobody understood, he was a heretic burning in a bonfire, fanning the executioner's rage by enduring in his silence and his truth.

II

I'D FIRST MET ALIOSCHA three years earlier, during one of the darkest periods in his life, when Élene had just left him and he was writing the first pages of *Attila*, living a lonely, painful existence in the Oberkampf apartment. Our meeting, and the alliance that would last until his death, came about thanks to an article I'd planned to write for the April issue of *El Paseante*, that as well as one of my many lapses regarding how I organized my work. It was a heady time rife with the near constant emergence of new literary talent, and I intended to reflect on the writers who had burst onto the scene over the course of the past decade. At first, I thought I might include Alioscha, who had published one book at that point, although—owing to number of authors to choose from and the need to be selective—I ultimately elected to leave him out. He had already received my first letter in which I invited him to be interviewed, when I had to write a second note of apology that included the promise of another interview in the future. To this second letter, Alioscha replied with an unusual approach, not demanding more exposure, as authors are wont to do, but wanting to contextualize some of the comments

I'd made about his work. *The book isn't some innovative experiment*—he clarified in response to the few lines I'd written about *Vital ventura saeculi*, his only novel at that point, which I'd considered an attempt as indecipherable and contrived as its title was unpronounceable. *To the contrary: it could almost be a classic Greek tragedy, depending on how you read it.*

The letter surprised me, mostly because of the care Alioscha appeared to take when considering my scant opinions, so trite and common they could have been about any novel at all, except one that actually interested me. That was the truth: not only had I *not* enjoyed his book, not in the least, but I'd also found it irritating, excessively difficult to understand, burdened with formal excesses and lacking in a clear plot. The fact was that I hadn't considered him for my article based on my faith in the trajectory of his writing career, but for other reasons, such as his publisher—the press with its finger on the pulse of young authors—as well as Alioscha's closeness in age to other writers I planned to review, and because I thought the person responsible for such an extravagant text might offer a unique perspective that could potentially bring attention to the feature. But his second letter, contrary to what one might expect from such a singular writer, was full of reasoned arguments, so intelligent and well-supported that I was obliged to reconsider many of my earlier judgments. And besides, his tone was cordial, with humility and care far removed from any kind of acrimony. Though I was pressed for time, I wrote back, a long and detailed message as pleasant and warm as his own letter had been, although I was honest with him, citing what I saw as the work's defects and not hiding the reasons I considered his efforts a beautiful but misguided attempt. Our peculiar epistolary exchange didn't end there. Not only did he remain unswayed by my convincing objections, but by some absurd logic they appeared to reaffirm his initial approach and lead him to conclusions as surprising as they were incontestable: *Some see a perfect mechanism present in the novel, an expression of intelligence, a kind of cerebral artifact*—Alioscha noted in that letter, with erudite quotes and references that impressed me. *But to me, it's nothing but an object, water and clay: a handicraft.*

After that, we developed a close friendship through regular correspondence that often included more than a letter a week. I quickly discovered that Alioscha was a peculiar reader with deep knowledge of the classics and absolute disinterest in the writers of his time. His confessions soon strayed beyond the literary. Unprompted, Alioscha began to broach personal subjects, like the troubles with his wife or his dependence on the family fortune, sudden and intimate revelations that were slightly embarrassing for two people who had never even met in person. All of his letters contained at least one autobiographical reference. He didn't complain, but relayed to me the many things he'd had to renounce as a writer, as well as the first lines he'd written as a boy, now forgotten and turned to ash, and listed several novels crucial to his development as a reader, novels he claimed to have devoured dozens of times, and even told me how once, during one grueling summer, he grew pale and thin in his zeal to finish a three-hundred page novel in one sitting. He also confessed other, more recent weaknesses, like his need to exhaust himself walking in order to combat the terrible insomnia that kept him awake for nights on end, or the sudden urge to cry over the deafening silence that had invaded his home. In one of his later missives, when I'd already let him know that—thanks to an assignment for the magazine—I would soon visit Paris and we could talk as much as he liked, Alioscha elaborated—over the course of three full pages—on the difficulties he had combining his writing with personal relationships, making very specific references to his marriage to Élene, tormented as he was by her threats to leave. *It's not the first time she's packed her bags*, he wrote. *She packs and unpacks, and she always says the same thing: that I won't be able to hold her prisoner for another week.*

Maybe the bits about Élene were a cry for help, or so they seemed to me, but I never did get the chance to bolster his spirits, since the breakup had already occurred by the time I first shook his hand in a tourist-filled café near the Place de la Bastille. He'd made no mention of the separation, however, during our brief phone chat the night before, even though I called him once I'd settled into my hotel and spoke warmly and intimately, inviting him his confidences. But Alioscha had replied matter-of-factly, ignoring all references to personal affairs, as if, despite the way he aired grievances in his letters, the only thing of any concern to him now was to ensure that there was no confusion about our meeting place.

He was anxious that there would be some last-minute mistake.

"If you get lost, go back to the metro," he said, reminding again me of the designated time and place. "If you haven't arrived by eleven-thirty, I'll look for you there."

Although he'd given me precise instructions, he must have turned up quite a bit beforehand, since when I arrived at the café at eleven o'clock on the dot—the agreed-upon time—his coffee cup was already empty. It was impossible to mistake him amid the bustle of the café. He had the tense, vigilant look of someone who had been waiting for someone a long time, feigning false calm but so impatient he couldn't keep his eyes off the door. When the long-awaited moment arrived and I stepped inside and waved to him, Alioscha was so flustered that he couldn't contain his nerves and stood up so hastily that he almost knocked over the table.

"Today is one of my few days off," he said, shaking my hand. Then, dispensing with the usual greetings and small talk: "I finished the second chapter of *Attila*."

It was the first time I heard him speak without the static of a long-distance call. His voice contained a cinematographic resonance, deep and very clear, though with a slow, removed quality that gave him an absent air. Everything about him lent that impression, anomalous and solemn, an oddness that was, nonetheless, disinterested in drawing attention to itself. He was wearing writer's clothes, but a writer from another era, like he had dressed up in the garb of poets from decades past: a white hankie tucked in his pocket and a narrow black jacket, classically cut, that might have easily been inherited from his grandfather. He had the look of a stranger in the land, glancing about with wonder, his eyes wide and expectant, as if permanently dazed, and his speech was likewise serious and measured, full of hesitation, as if he was unused to being among people.

Alioscha proved his social awkwardness shortly after we began talking, when I observed out loud that they'd brought my coffee without sugar. He hurried to rectify the mistake, calling loudly to the waiter clear across the room. The man attended to us with a censorious look, gruffly making it clear that he'd prefer that we vacated the table as soon as possible.

But Alioscha, indifferent to the waiter's indignation, went on as if nothing had happened, and made a passing comment about his relationship with Élene.

"She disappeared one night, just like that. No explanation except a note on the dining room table." He seemed much less afflicted than in his letters. "She came yesterday with a gallerist friend to collect some of her clothes and other things she couldn't take with her the night she fled."

Alioscha gave no further details about the incident. Certainly not on account of the fresh sting of the memory, which undoubtedly still pained him, nor an unexpected compunction in a person as transparent as he was, but because he was instead eager to talk about the early pages of his novel.

"This is the outline," he whispered, unfolding a piece of paper with hieroglyphic notations so strange they looked like notes arranged on a sheet of music. "If I spend two months on each chapter, the book will be finished in a little under three years."

Alioscha went on to explain that he'd long had the custom of devising an elaborate cartography of his books, differentiating the main scenes from secondary ones and highlighting the most poetic passages, just as he always handwrote the first draft in his old-fashioned penmanship, only typing the final text later, once he'd achieved a clean manuscript. He told me that more than once he'd spend a whole morning on a single sentence, changing every verb and every adjective time and again, endlessly trying out new solutions, only to opt for the original version, unable to move on if a single word wasn't to his satisfaction. He worked so much and with such devotion and felt such a sense of responsibility that he could go weeks without leaving his room, barely getting up from his desk, engaged in battle with some lethal paragraph. Not one day went by when he had a single minute to spare, he claimed.

"It's even worse now," he said, referring to the changes that had taken effect since his wife left. "Sometimes I eat all my meals at my desk."

That first visit, more was revealed than what he told me in his own words, such as his tumultuous relationship with his father, Bartomeu. I found myself witness to their dynamic that very day, right around noon. Shortly after we left the café, Alioscha insisted I join him at his apartment to look over some pages of his novel. He eagerly planned to share a few paragraphs from the latest chapter, finished just hours before we met. His excitement was palpable and suggested a desire to gauge my reaction, to validate whether he had really captured moments of inspired musicality or if it was merely a passing illusion.

We walked in the direction of his apartment, engrossed in a conversation about dead writers, forgotten books, and literary myths of bygone eras, until we came to his front door. Just as he was about to put the key in the lock, we heard murmuring voices that gave us pause. These were the tense exchanges between his cousin and father, apparently on the other side of the door and in the midst of hashing out a plan to address the "Alioscha situation."

Regardless of what their original strategy had been, it was rendered inconsequential when Alioscha opened the door and Bartomeu rushed toward his son, foregoing any sociable greeting. "We explicitly told you that we were coming today, and we expected you to be here at noon," he declared sharply, delivering a less-than-affectionate slap to Alioscha's cheek. "We arrived on time, but the doorwoman had to let us in."

Alioscha, who just seconds before had been elated at the prospect of sharing his narrative concerns, went stiff and serious.

"I thought your flight got in at noon," he started to explain, trying to make eye contact with his cousin. "I assumed you wouldn't come by until after lunch."

But his father continued to rebuke him, keeping a hand on his shoulder and shaking his head in disapproval. He stood inches from Alioscha's face.

"This is how you've been your whole life—messing up dates, being in the wrong place, forgetting your commitments," he admonished, looking at Alioscha intensely. "All you had to do was write down the details of our visit on a piece of paper."

The conversation quickly turned into an unpleasant confrontation, revealing the deep-seated resentment they harbored for one another. It was one of many clashes, and I witnessed firsthand how Bartomeu addressed Alioscha with a complete lack of empathy. Not even the news of his son's recent marital woes could temper his harsh words. On the contrary, he declared Alioscha to be the family's biggest disgrace, recounting instances of his clumsiness and absent-mindedness dating back to childhood. Like a distant afternoon when Alioscha left the oven on, resulting a small fire, and multiple occasions when, as a child, he had left the house in mismatched shoes, returning home in tears after being teased by his classmates.

Bartomeu also critiqued the state of Alioscha's clothes during his lengthy diatribe. Old and tattered, he declared, and cuttingly interrupted his son's attempts to defend himself, expressing his fury that a man over forty still couldn't take care of himself like an adult. It struck me that Bartomeu had very little in common with Alioscha. Not only did the man exude self-assuredness, maintaining steady eye contact and striding about, but father and son were starkly different in their physical appearance. Bartomeu, a vain man, dressed in a jacket and colorful tie with impeccably styled hair and beard, enjoyed a seemingly permanent tan. Every gesture reflected his meticulous and sophisticated bearing, a far cry from any semblance of vulgarity. His presence contrasted sharply with the disastrous state of Alioscha's apartment—a sparely decorated space with wilting plants and a long-neglected Christmas tree, littered with used towels and dirty plates.

His son's living conditions were unfathomable to him:

"Only an animal, or drunkard spurning society, could live like this," he criticized, recoiling at the unpleasant smell in the kitchen. "It's like you were raised in a barn."

In an attempt to gather more ammunition against his son, Bartomeu inspected every room systematically. Closets, drawers, and even the upturned corners of rugs were scrutinized, the articles of rumpled clothing noted. He singled out the chaotic jumble of pants and sweaters, demanding that Alioscha organize them on the spot. His scorn intensified when he ridiculed his son for the lack of a broom in the pantry and the inexcusable act of keeping expired milk in the refrigerator. Fed up with picking up broken bottles and crumpled papers from the floor, Bartomeu returned to the living room. There, he stopped before two of Élene's unfinished canvases, appreciating her use of color and delicate brushstrokes with an expert eye.

"This place was obviously unbearable for her," he mused, turning his back on Alioscha while closely examining the paintings. "No wonder she left—she got sick of putting up with someone like you. She was too good for you."

At these words, Alioscha finally erupted in rage. Reflecting his father's ferocity, he hurled accusations, portraying Bartomeu as an obtuse and unremarkable man—an idle and talentless heir who had achieved nothing substantial in almost seventy years, a simple perpetuator of the old family ways. Alioscha smashed a flowerpot, and nearly tripped as he tore a canvas off the wall. He cursed his wife's paintings before moving to make a defiant exit, pausing on the stairs and growling a final defiant sentence:

"You're the one who looks like a savage—at a museum or in an opera box. Today you clap for the same things you would've rejected had you been born a few years earlier."

Following Alioscha's dramatic exit, I found myself unexpectedly accepting lunch in the company of his father and cousin.

Bartomeu selected a small and elegant restaurant without tourists, where, over the course of three hours, he showcased his conversational skills, seeking common interests and reminiscing about his youthful adventures abroad. When the first course arrived, I mentioned my work as a frequent contributor to a literary magazine, covering reviews and features on current affairs. Bartomeu dove right into the latest literary trends, clearly *au courant*. He transitioned seamlessly into a discussion of the visual arts and listed the various operas he planned to attend in the coming year.

Bartomeu's deftness went beyond highbrow subjects, as he expertly described the virtues of the wine he'd chosen and later digressed on the different techniques used by Galician and Norman fishermen. As we were about to leave, Bartomeu bid farewell to the restaurant's manager with gestures that would have been impossible for Alioscha: a generous tip, an effusive handshake, and even advice on perfecting one of the desserts we'd been served.

Whether or not his expertise extended to the realm of patisserie, he behaved like the sociable and refined man he actually was, and only returned to the subject of his son as we were taking our leave.

"It doesn't matter how hard he works," he concluded with feigned disgust. "It doesn't matter how much he writes or how much he reads. It doesn't matter how bad he wants it. No one will ever want to read a single page written by a man like him."

Carlos Valls, Alioscha's more understanding relative, protested at Bartomeu's harsh words and rushed to recount an anecdote that demonstrated Alioscha's brilliance and expressed admiration for his cousin.

"But it is true, you know, what Bartomeu says," Valls remarked as we parted ways, his ironic smile directed only at me. "And Alioscha himself might even be aware of it: sometimes I think he knows that he's talking to himself in a desert, yet somehow he's conscious that the inadequacy of words is better than silence."

Regardless of who was right, we three bid each other a cordial farewell, pledging to keep an eye on the precarious path Alioscha seemed to be treading.

As for me, I quickly discovered more facets of my new friend's mysterious personality. In fact, the very next morning, the day before my scheduled flight home, when I was already sure I wouldn't see him again for a long time, Alioscha called my room. Despite the cool touch of the receiver and the interference of the cables, his voice sounded close and affectionate, as if a sudden complicity had been established between us.

"We have to meet again," he said, omitting any mention of the altercation with Bartomeu. "There's still time for me to show you my latest chapter."

It was a clumsy excuse. Alioscha simply wanted to return to the peace we had enjoyed before his father's intrusion. And so we did. Instead of focusing on his drafts, which he didn't even bring with him, we spent the whole afternoon walking aimlessly, no destination in mind. It felt both automatic and happenstance, reminiscent of those movie scenes in which survivors wander the ruins of a deserted city. Everything we did seemed to respond to Alioscha's poetic impulses.

He suggested we look at secondhand books along the Seine, and we headed there to sift through cracked and dusty copies, discovering out-of-print novels. We caused a stir among the booksellers, taking copies from the tables and reading aloud long passages that excited us. Alioscha was a flamboyant public speaker. With passion and skill, he recited from classic texts, whether Russian novels or beloved Elizabethan plays, waving his hands and tossing his hair as if on stage. His dramatic reading drew a small crowd of curious onlookers who mistook him for a street poet and were even prepared to toss him a coin.

Once we'd distanced ourselves from that accidental commotion, Alioscha was plunged into one of his mythical reveries that would later become so familiar to me. It happened abruptly, for no apparent reason, as he stopped short in the middle of the business-lined street and changed direction. Practically at a run, he led me to a small vacant lot, claiming that over a century ago, a bloody duel between writers had taken place there—a tragic account of oaths sworn at dawn and long, smoking pistols, a tale he seemed to mold according to his whims. That wasn't his only flight of fancy that day. After a brief pause in a square across from the Louvre, Alioscha spotted a young woman with a braid, a street vendor selling trinkets and postcards. He watched her wordlessly for a few minutes, seemingly drawn by an irresistible force. Against my advice, he approached her with the foolish intention of asking her out on a date. As expected, the street vendor's response was dismissive.

"She told me she only talks to customers for work, so I had to buy something," he said, disappointed by the rejection and stroking a ceramic figurine. "One for five francs and two for eight."

Despite the girl's rejection, Alioscha remained happy, his face radiant, his gaze intense and bright. In the middle of the sidewalk, he enthusiastically told anecdotes in a buoyant voice, in stark contrast to the livid man I had seen in the debris of his apartment the day before. Yet even in this confident state, far from his incessant depressive fogs, the moment I mentioned his father, Alioscha's expression turned grave. He swiftly put a stop to the conversation with a conclusive statement, possessed, perhaps, by a hostile memory that erased the happiness from his eyes.

"To him, literature is like good china," Alioscha said, kicking a plastic bag skittering down the sidewalk. "Something shiny and pretty to display in the living room."

Once the words left his mouth, Alioscha's mood shifted again, becoming calmer, more melancholy, as if preoccupied by the dark quiet of the falling night. Nevertheless, there was nothing to stop us from continuing on our peculiar journey as drifting amblers. Without planning our return or discussing how we'd get back, not even when the first streetlights blinked on, we escaped the city traffic and continued our ramble along the river, leaving churches, museums, and wide, congested avenues behind until we reached one of the most famous bridges over the Seine, where we stopped at the midpoint.

It was one of the best possible times of day—eight o'clock in the evening, an hour of waning sunlight and soon-to-be farewells. The dusky end of the day when birds went mad in the sky and on street corners music hung in the air with languid slowness. Everything seemed submerged in a strange sense of ending, and every movement and every utterance contained the hint of strange yet routine death. Even the Seine itself appeared under the hour's influence. There was an intense light, a strong horizontal thrust, and from bank to bank the waters shone in smooth and uniform combinations, like sheets of steel. The stillness was broken only by the slow and expectant passing of the tourist boats, with their weak electric glow and a tinkling of glasses and murmur of voices signaling that dinner was about to be served onboard.

In the atmosphere of calm seclusion and secret intimacy there in the heart of the city, Alioscha and I watched as one of the huge recreational boats appeared below our feet. Its course was unhurried, like the others, but it was empty, with no visible passengers on deck. It sailed downriver, northward, awash in its own twilight, flags lowered and lamps still unlit, a ghost ship. An old boat with a hull full of dents and dings, its course appeared even more listless. All the forces of the evening seemed to converge there, on that vessel reminiscent of a defeated galleon, battered from so much sailing, no remaining will except to reach the shores of a peaceful ocean, graze the sea spray with its tin body, and carry out its ritual of sinking, coming to rest forever in the immensity of an underwater valley.

Alioscha watched the vessel until it disappeared in the winding of the current, and it seemed to me that he might have been imagining the boat's resemblance to himself, lungs filled with smoke and poor air, chest wracked by many unrealized dreams.

"If I ever stopped writing," he said in one of his overwrought confessions I sometimes found intimidating, being unused to such innocence and sincerity at once. "That might be the solution: find a bridge like this one, and a ship to leave on forever."

DURING THOSE EARLY MONTHS of our friendship, nearly three years before my friend's demise, certain enduring patterns were established. After the visit that had coincided with Élene leaving him, Alioscha's cousin Carlos Valls became my regular confidant. We got together a few weeks later in Madrid, where he tried to justify his visit with the flimsy excuse of a professional meeting but spent the whole time delving into his cousin's quietly epic story. We shared a classic Madrid cocido in a tavern in the city center while discussing Élene's escape, her previous crises with Alioscha, and Valls's attempts to excuse his uncle's callousness by underscoring the trouble his son caused. Real confidences emerged as we strolled the wide sidewalks of the Palacio del Oriente. Valls handed me a book of poems he'd penned, acknowledging that he, too, once dreamt of becoming an author, but settled for writing only on the weekends.

I began to see the parallels—and divergences—between Carlos Valls's life and that of his cousin. Valls revealed that his interest in writing developed at the same time as Alioscha's, during one formative summer when they both sought summits where they could duel with death. While both young men read the same number of books, Valls embraced writing with a less visceral impulse, avoiding its totalizing fire. Alioscha, with his romantic nature marked by innocence and a rejection of his upbringing, battled relentlessly.

"He was the same with writing as he might have been with a pair of combat boots and a machine gun in the jungle."

As we made our way down the promenade, Valls recounted stories that illustrated Alioscha's obsessive nature and their diverging life decisions. During his student days, Alioscha's eccentricities included adopting an unusual sleep regimen and organizing purges of his oldest novels, burning them in purifying bonfires on the beach. Valls mentioned Alioscha's ascetic isolation during those years, as he became mired in eccentricities and sublimated all about age-appropriate desires and concerns in service of his literary dream.

"He was like a monk at twenty."

Valls described Alioscha's peculiar apprenticeship, which involved typing out classic texts word for word: an absurd copyist's exercise not unlike mimicking a work of art by a genius painter.

"He filled entire folders with those crazy imitations."

Over the course of the evening, Valls talked about Alioscha with pride and admiration coupled with the sorrowful awareness that his cousin's noble struggle might well lead him to the edge of madness. As we said our goodbyes, Valls invoked Alioscha's voluntary exile in Paris and expressed the premonition that his cousin's efforts might well be the death of him. But at least it would be a worthy death, he said, as if Alioscha were fighting against some vague dictator, torch in hand.

It was also a veiled reference to Valls's own situation, to the many dreams he'd already discarded before the age of forty, and to how difficult it was for someone like to him to give any sort of advice to a man like his cousin.

"He'd keep on even if he were sure that he wouldn't succeed, that he'd face failure in the end," he remarked with a small laugh, acknowledging the naivety of his metaphor. "Picture him traipsing through the mountains, firing shots into the wind. You can't expect a man like that to come back to civilization."

While Valls's revelations shed light on his cousin's enduring vocation, the loneliness of his teenage years, and the rigorous apprenticeship he'd subjected himself to before writing his books, I found I was familiar with some of those details already, as they'd been shared by Alioscha himself in the written correspondence we resumed upon my return to Madrid. I had frequent news of him by post, and over time, that, in addition to parallel conversations with his cousin and my visits to the French capital, led to my growing fascination with the man with the prophetic air who engaged in quiet yet tempestuous deeds. My visits to Paris were always brief, often disguised as conveniently timed interviews with Latin American novelists passing through the City of Light, though on other occasions there was no excuse at all, and I invented farfetched reasons to explain my interest in Alioscha, in hopes he wouldn't become suspicious.

All of our encounters, lasting until his death, followed a pattern similar to that of our first morning together. We'd meet around noon, by which time he had already done several hours of work. Despite any gastronomic plans I might have had, we tended to wind up at restaurants chosen by Alioscha—noisy, local places in his neighborhood. He dressed for the occasion in a style that was a blend of classic and careless, and usually included dirty shoes, mismatched socks, or a cracked watch face. Our restaurant outings also provided opportunities for Alioscha to steal napkins or silverware, and I encouraged him to indulge in foods he didn't allow himself when alone. I always settled the bill despite his attempts to pay, aware of his meager budget sustained by a small inheritance and sporadic contributions from his father.

And though I bought him meals and offered him pieces of practical advice, in no way did I view our friendship as a humanitarian mission. I didn't visit Alioscha out of obligation or charity, nor did I hope to find something interesting for future features in *El Paseante*. My reason for those trips was to understand the strange writing obsession he had suffered from for so long. Truly a man like no other, Alioscha possessed a lucid yet impenetrable mind, imbued with an epic disposition that suggested he had known Paris for a hundred years, as he wandered on long treks through narrow alleyways or around popular cemeteries.

His juvenile idolism sometimes led to uncomfortable situations. One November morning, after a long walk, we stopped at the statue of a famous writer. Alioscha, elated, asked a woman to take our picture with her own camera.

She hurried away, suspicious, as if she had been assaulted by pickpockets. In his elation, Alioscha couldn't understand the woman's suspicion of two men who smelled so strongly of wine.

"But I offered her twenty francs!" he insisted as we moved away from the tourists. "A lot more than she would have spent on stamps and developing the film."

Yes, in those years between his wife's departure and the start of his tortured affair with Camille, Alioscha had become a stranger among the living—a lost cause with no hope of redemption, unable to understand others' passions and problems, with a habit of veering unpredictably between emotions.

With each visit and letter, I delved deeper into his complex personality. He exhibited two distinct and opposing characters: the conscientious writer, responsible and tenacious with work habits like those of a civil servant, and the naive and imaginative man prone to intense and lasting excitement. Persistent signs of his fantastical inclinations surfaced. He used diverse methods to obtain novels he couldn't afford: if he borrowed books from the library, he altered the official stamped due dates, extending his possession by several weeks. In cases where his fondness for a book exceeded his willingness to part with it, he resorted to more extreme measures, carefully tearing out the most impactful and exemplary pages. Subsequently, he nervously returned the modified book to the library, his voice betraying his anxiety. There were also times when, despite his lack of stealth, he opted to steal from bookshops. I even found myself participating unwittingly in one such theft when one rainy day, while browsing a small shop, I watched Alioscha discreetly tuck a book under his jacket, prompting our hasty retreat, leaving the shop assistant confused as to why two respectable-looking adults were fleeing in terror down the street.

His unorthodox character manifested in many other situations, including his clandestine spying on a female neighbor, whom he observed getting out of the shower every day at the same time, glimpsing, through a sufficiently large gap in the blinds, her completely naked figure, clouded in steam. Despite the voyeuristic nature of the act, there was nothing lascivious in Alioscha's intention, as he was driven more by admiration for the hazy spectacle of her figure than by anything depraved. He even concocted a plan to approach her in the vestibule and present her with a bouquet of flowers.

His emotional fragility, evident in persistently awkward situations, led to other romantic setbacks. His innocent tactics of seduction included giving a waitress a book with his phone number written inside, then nervously sitting on his couch for a week, awaiting a late-night call. One sunny morning, he recited a French poem to a group of young women we were passing on a bridge. Taken by flights of fancy, he invited shopgirls he barely knew to dinner, only to face repeated rejections and bewilderment at their unexpectedly startled reactions.

And so, only a few months after meeting him, I already understood Alioscha's principal affliction: an overwhelming sense of loneliness. This led him to fall in and out of infatuation, capable of becoming obsessed with any Parisian student just because their paths had crossed that morning. His cousin and I were dismayed to discover he made random phone calls to unknown women; numbers drawn from the thousands of names in the Paris phone book. There was even an incident where he was punched by a husband whose wife he pursued in the man's presence.

We both understood the impact loneliness was having on his health and his writing.

"I went into his room one day and thought he was sleeping," Valls shared in a poignant example. "He was whispering a conversation, an oneiric dialogue in which he apparently played his own part first and then imitated a woman's voice, acting out both sides of a dialogue."

I agreed, noting how it sometimes seemed that he needed to close his eyes and hear his own made-up sounds in order to survive, finding comfort from silence in his hallucinations.

Valls took it further, linking the absolute emptiness of Alioscha's life under the gray Parisian skies to the darkness present in his books, a pained assertion he appeared to have given lengthy consideration.

"This is why no one will ever be able to understand his work: unintentionally, unknowingly, imperceptibly, they are written for him and him alone," he said slowly, as if frightened by his own conclusions. "It's like he's been lost for years among the beasts of the jungle and finally had to invent his own language."

His thesis might well have been correct. By then Alioscha had been trapped, irremediably, in a hellish circle for many years: he had poured so much effort into writing that he'd become deaf and blind to everything else, estranged from his surroundings, so disoriented when faced with the frenzy of the world that his work was destined for the most consolidated hermeticism. There was no better proof than the contradictory feelings his texts always produced. His writing sought risk and innovation, and contained sentences that suddenly rose to solemn heights, so lofty they seemed destined to live on, as if, instead of words strung together, they were pieces of ruins that had always been there, waiting to be rescued. Yet, no matter how many preliminary outlines he attempted, there was always a lack of coherence, of clear intention, of some well-defined idea or consistent argument—more consistent, at least, than the frayed threads one had to struggle to pull together, page after page, trying to make some kind of whole. His writings were so delirious that I often felt like the words that comprised them had gotten shaken up in the mail sacks on the flight to Spain and were thus out of order upon their arrival in my letterbox. I even found myself examining pages on which there were sentences consisting of a simple repetition of the same word, like some typographical error, although Alioscha defended the artistic freedom of those surprising pages. I delicately pointed out all these eccentricities to him, inviting him to write something simpler, though by the time I met him, he was incapable of understanding my opinions, lost in abysses so private they impeded him from hearing any advice.

Emotionally adrift, his personal life didn't inspire much optimism either. Months after his wife fled, Alioscha was still far from forgetting her, missing her more desperately than ever, the signs of his instability even greater than what I'd been told he suffered during their final weeks together. There was nothing in him to show that he understood it was better to live free from the earlier tension with Élene. On the contrary, instead of falling into a colorless ennui—as often comes about in such situations—and retreating from all the uncertainty, his behavior became more extreme, for good and bad: you were just as likely to find him exuberant over any quotidian incident, cheery and even ebullient in his routine, as to find him sunk in deep chasms of sorrow. That capacity for exaltation enabled him to thrill over any old pretext, such as winter's first snow on the Paris rooftops, or because a waitress in a café was wearing the same *eau de cologne* that his wife had worn. But more revealing than those eruptions of gaiety was his demonstrable longing to be with someone, which caused him to fumble cups and plates in restaurants, overcome by nerves, or to linger in the hotel doorway the night his cousin Carlos Valls or I landed, tired of the conversations with his own reflection in the mirrors in the Oberkampf apartment. The deterioration of his person was perceptible from a distance, as well. Some nights he called me in Madrid at ungodly hours, when he needed it most, and once or twice he even rang just minutes after hanging up, with some thin excuse, trying to resume a conversation that in reality was already finished, clinging to the fragile companionship of my distant voice before confronting the emptiness he found every night between his sheets.

Like me, his cousin Carlos Valls believed Alioscha's eccentricities had intensified during that period. On the trips he took to Paris over the course of those months, Valls surprised Alioscha in implausible situations, buoyant after buying a few flowerpots, or disconsolate after failing to locate some of Élene's old scarves at the back of the armoire. Yet what really caused an impression, what scared him to the point of realizing that he was in fact witnessing a certain harbinger of doom, was when he caught Alioscha engaged in a practice imbued with a certain secretive air, scribbling paragraphs of his novel in vertical verse on the living room wallpaper, marking the wall with quick, determined strokes, like graffiti.

It was upon returning to Barcelona and relaying to me what he'd seen that Valls conveyed his intention to put a stop to that nonsense.

"We can't wait any longer," he said. "Either we get him out of Paris soon or we start looking for a plot in one of those cemeteries he loves visiting so much."

His plan consisted of drawing Alioscha to Barcelona with the pretext of a family reunion, and once he was there, to try and keep him captive and away from the solitary mire of his condemned-man's apartment. Part of Valls's exercise in persuasion would be to promise Alioscha that he would only have to coincide with his father for one short night, at the dinner to be held at Valls's home in Castelldefels, which meant that Alioscha could enjoy the rest of the days by the sea and its calm horizons, with no worries except keeping sand out of his shoes. Then, Valls would subtly present him with an option for renouncing his self-imposed Parisian exile, so that Alioscha might accept the proposal of returning to

Barcelona without the sense that anybody had forced him into it.

"I'll tell him that he has two jobs available here, neither of which will slow down the writing of his book," Valls said, explaining that his father agreed to grant him the exclusive use of a studio in the city center. "One is to write sporadic articles for a newspaper supplement, and the other is to pretend that he's helping me with patients one morning a week."

Over the course of the following days, I heard about the conversations in which Valls tried to convince Alioscha. I followed along, intrigued, waiting for news, though I was skeptical of the outcome, sure that Alioscha would never give up his self-imposed exile, and was thus surprised when Valls called to assure me that, after several futile attempts, his cousin had finally yielded.

"Now I just need his father to control himself," he sighed, indicating that Bartomeu was aware of the plan. "I've asked him to sit down at a table with his son without it ending in smashed plates for once in their lives."

In the weeks leading up to his trip to Spain, I maintained my routine chats with Alioscha, combining literary debates and personal confessions, and even received several pages of his novel by mail, but he never made any mention of the plans for his brief return to his place of origin. Perhaps he chose to keep his sojourn secret because he suspected that a hidden trap was set, or perhaps he kept quiet out of some inexpressible sense of shame, convinced that giving himself three days' rest in the middle of the writing process represented an unjustifiable form of weakness. In any case, thanks to Valls's detailed accounts, I knew that he and Alioscha had greeted one another with a warm embrace, and that a few hours after meeting in the airport arrivals hall, they'd eaten with Valls's wife and daughters at a beachfront restaurant and in a buoyant atmosphere that gave Valls hope.

"We just might manage it," he reported after barely half a day spent together, when I asked about the status of his project. "He didn't get upset when my wife told him that leaving Paris was the best way to forget Élene."

Yet just two days later, all faith that his cousin might be converted into a balanced, moderate man who worked in the mornings and wrote in the afternoons had vanished.

It was the day after the dinner party, the only time Alioscha had been in the same room as his father, and it was easy to imagine what had transpired.

"He left this morning. Without a goodbye. Without telling me: as if I were Bartomeu's accomplice, all for having put him up in a room overlooking the Mediterranean."

His concern was understandable. Saddened by the suddenness of Alioscha's departure, Valls assured me that his cousin had spent the first and second days of his stay happy and relaxed, influenced by the clarity of the light and calming rhythms of the waves, with an ease and confidence that reminded Valls of a scorching August in childhood when the two cousins had completely dedicated themselves to catching crabs in the tidepools. Alioscha had seemed so content, so comforted by his return to the forgotten places of bygone summers, that he'd even talked about childhood friends they had in common, and asked whereabouts in the city they lived and what they did for work, as if he was willing to forget the scars inflicted in other times and reconcile with the past once and for all.

"He spent his mornings by the sea, on the deserted February beaches, showing my daughters how to anticipate the waves as they rolled in and out, and his nights with me and my wife, over long dinners, doing impressions of Bartomeu and joking about his unrequited teenage romances," said Valls, clearly disappointed that his ruse had ended so poorly.

After meals, Alioscha took advantage of the quiet to dust off some of the tricks he had forgotten with time, such as knack remembering the surnames of every classmate, or his erstwhile skills as a magician, as he boasted of being able to use a deck of cards to determine whether or not a couple was still in love. It was precisely during one of those prolonged after-lunch conversations that Valls raised the possibility of ending the chosen exile that had taken him to Paris. It happened one afternoon, during the siesta, high on a terrace overlooking the sea, which spread before them like an endless slate expanse. Valls took advantage of the fact that everyone else was resting to change the topic of conversation, and cautiously suggested the benefits of working a few hours and living a comfortably paced life in an apartment in central Barcelona.

"He listened calmly until I was done, but then refused, obviously feeling no need to justify himself," Valls continued, now speaking closer into the mouthpiece, recreating for me the open space of the sunlit terrace, wounded because he still didn't have a firm grasp of what had gone wrong with his cousin. "He smiled—genuinely—as if my proposal amused him, and even laughed, joking that we could write a novel together when things were quiet at the clinic."

But Valls also acknowledged that deep down he knew there was something incorruptible in Alioscha, the mark of a warrior, a passion for struggle and resistance that precluded moderation, just as he knew that Bartomeu would never accept his son's eccentricities, and thus conceded that there was nothing remarkable about the conflict that boiled over between them in front of the dozen people around the table.

"It all started with Bartomeu's comment about a famous Catalan writer who had just published a novel after decades as a successful professor. Bartomeu claimed that the man's accomplishment was in no way inferior to that of the many other high-profile poets who slogged through life as waiters or hotel receptionists," he continued, not needing to explain the significance of the malicious remark. "Alioscha didn't react at first, but when he did, it was by chucking his napkin down on his full plate, banging his spoon against his glass, and ticking off a long list of authors who had always lived in obscurity, only redeemed by their difficult yet brilliant works and saved from the calamities of fate once they were in the grave."

Valls sighed thoughtfully on the other end of the line, unsettled perhaps by the mere memory of what followed. He spared no detail in his description of the ensuing dispute yet couldn't help but show the displeasure it had caused him. "Bartomeu accused Alioscha of the very worst thing: of having become a coward, of hiding behind that façade of future, posthumous glory to avoid facing his present shortcomings. And Alioscha, unable to contain himself any longer, responded by insulting his father in every possible way before he stood up from the table, yelling and knocking over his chair, and left the house. He simply couldn't be calmed."

Valls then went on to detail the bitter scene in the wake of his cousin's departure, no longer hiding his anger toward Bartomeu, who had insisted on carrying on with dinner. "My uncle was still disparaging Alioscha, so I left immediately and went to look for him around the estate and out by the yachts in the marina under the bright lights of the docks—and in the water. I only gave up after I'd combed all the nearby streets and beaches and decided to wait for him at home on the couch, until I fell asleep. I woke at sunrise and went straight to his bedroom, hoping to catch him before he'd packed his suitcase, to convince him to calm down and keep the promise he made to demonstrate his kite flying skills to the girls before he left."

But Valls didn't find him then, in the pale morning light filtering in through the windows, nor in the hours that followed, because while he slept on the couch, Alioscha had snuck off to the airport in time to catch a flight home, spurred more by the anxiety provoked by a possible conversation about the fight at dinner than by fear of missing his plane.

"Apparently, he avoided talking to anyone by climbing in and out through the window," Valls concluded before we hung up, describing his cousin's burglar-like tactics. "He took the clothes and books I'd lent him and left me a note apologizing for getting up from the table when he still had food on his plate."

TWO WEEKS AFTER HE quietly fled Castelldefels, Alioscha suffered the first disastrous consequence: Bartomeu, fed up with his son's obstinacy, sick of what he considered his mistakes, decided not to make his usual monthly contribution, therefore ensuring that Alioscha could no longer keep up his charade as a misunderstood writer in Paris at the expense of Bartomeu's savings. He made the decision, however, without consulting or warning anyone, not even his son, and so Alioscha called him on the first Monday in March, convinced that the usual deposit had been delayed. Only then did his father inform him that, until Alioscha made the return trip to Spain, he would no longer be underwriting his expenses:

"Go ahead and drown in your books, stroll along the Seine. But if you want to write, you'll have to work, or learn to catch pigeons to feed yourself."

His son replied angrily, with an equally threatening message, incredulous that his father hadn't warned him:

"You go ahead and eat for me," he shouted, furious, humiliated by the sudden feeling of dependence. "In the meantime,

I'll create for the both of us, so you can keep going to parties and gallery openings."

It was another family cataclysm. Learning of this new feud, Valls contacted Alioscha in hopes of making him see Bartomeu's legitimate reasons for concern, based not so much on a fear of eschewing social norms as his responsibility as a guardian, and trying to find a middle ground that would prevent an even more serious rift. He begged him to behave sensibly, urging him to consider an alternative to his stubborn exile, arguing that there was a way to live that was free and personal, authentic and brave, in which he could keep writing, of course, and with the utmost ambition, but without succumbing to degrading excesses. But no matter how numerous and varied his arguments, Valls could find no way to redirect Alioscha. It was no wonder. Alioscha simply could not understand what it meant to undertake a venture only halfway, without being completely consumed in the effort, and according to his peculiar inner logic, what was dignified and true and passionate consisted of persevering in his hermit-like isolation in Paris, immune to all temptation, oblivious to the glitter and lies of literary glory, convinced that anything other than staying put in his chair at his wobbly-legged desk was a shameful form of surrender. He didn't even hesitate when presented with Valls's tempting assurances that, if he returned to Barcelona, he could work on his novel at the hospital, getting paid per diem with no obligations other than following the schedule, and he even promised to set him up in a cozy office with good light, where he could write with no demands from anyone for anything.

But Alioscha refused, turning his cousin's logic around.

"That would be like begging on a church doorstep, except instead of kneeling with my hand out, I'd have to wear a name tag and white coat."

After several refusals, Valls accepted that Alioscha could not be convinced, and that the more he encouraged his cousin to return, the less likely it was to happen, since he knew Alioscha always rebelled against any manner of bribery. So he switched to a much less ambitious goal: instead of worrying about how far away Paris was from Barcelona, he focused on more basic concerns, like ensuring that Alioscha kept his dignity and didn't have to scrounge for food or deprive himself of the occasional coffee out.

"When he was eleven, Alioscha was punished by not being allowed to go to the beach because he threw an ice cream wrapper on the ground outside the trash can," he explained. "He accepted and didn't complain, but then refused to swim for the whole month: he spent all of August scouring the sidewalks looking for those same wrappers until he filled two big bags."

Before he hung up, Valls also mentioned that he had requested two days' leave to fly to Paris, concerned about his cousin's potential reaction to being cut off financially and believing him capable of relying on pigeons as his only food source just because Bartomeu had challenged him to it. His trip couldn't have been timelier: the moment he saw him, Valls confirmed with alarm that Alioscha had completely neglected everything outside of writing, to such a degree that Valls couldn't restrain himself from offering urgent advice. On finding Alioscha so pale and thin, so deteriorated in the span of just two weeks, Valls promoted the benefits of a more dynamic routine, alternating physical exercise with intellectual work, so that in addition to cobbling together long subordinate clauses, Alioscha might also try moving his stiff limbs. His main recommendations, however, were of the domestic order: when he inspected the pantry and found nothing but bags of rice, a handful of soft, moldy potatoes, and a jar of cheap coffee, he encouraged Alioscha to broaden his gastronomic horizons. He took him to the fruit shop and the market, and even taught him how to fix himself broths and salads. He spent several hours helping his cousin with even more basic tasks, like opening the windows to rid the apartment of the stale air or unclogging the sink drains. Valls endeavored to address all the problems, and even created a checklist for when Alioscha was on his own again, writing down a series of instructions on a board that he stuck to the fridge to remind his cousin to eat a balanced diet and clean the house. Only when he was leaving, having battled dust mites and cobwebs and assured Alioscha that his trip hadn't been Bartomeu's idea, did Valls slide an envelope with one hundred francs across the table.

"It's yours, with just one condition," he said, looking at him seriously when Alioscha made a joke about his zealous scouring. "And that's that you tell me the second you run out of money."

But Alioscha never accepted even the subtlest of bribes, and Valls found the same envelope in his mailbox a few days later. Along with the money, Alioscha had included a damning note:

"I know you believe in me much more than he does," cautioned the curt message. "But deep down, you and my father have something in common: you want to put me in a cage, then tell me I can fly wherever I want."

Valls read those few lines with a heavy heart, dismayed by the distrust his cousin's words implied, and growing fearful that, going forward, Alioscha would treat him with resentment, or worse: that he would believe Valls had become a kind of agent, manipulated by Bartomeu's sinister puppet strings. Such suspicions were understandable, especially given that Bartomeu and his son had not yet reconciled after the dinner in Castelldefels.

"They're still the same," Valls informed me before leaving for the clinic, despairing over his relatives' mutual misunderstanding. "After a minute on the phone with his father, Alioscha either hangs up or they get bogged down in some bitter argument, recriminating each other from hundreds of kilometers away."

There was nothing new in that. Recalling childhood grievances or other more recent disputes, the only sure thing was that Alioscha and Bartomeu rejected each other just as staunchly as they always had. And my relationship with him showed no changes, either; while Alioscha persisted in feuding with his father, he and I continued to have very close contact, speaking frequently and exchanging letters once a week. I heard by his own account how his novel was progressing, or the status of his latest romantic failures, or if he had caught another glimpse of his neighbor in the nude. In one letter from that period, along with the confession that he'd been bewitched by a waitress of Latin origins at the place he now ate breakfast, he also included a few pages of a translation he had done of *Henry VIII* by Christopher Marlowe, whom he claimed to feel much closer to than any other novelist of his age. In his letter, he remarked that he'd started the translation because he found it a pleasant exercise, a perfect opportunity to surrender to the rhythmic cadences of verse drama, and because he believed it would allow him to enjoy an experience similar to that of an actor on stage: "When I translate, it's like I'm performing the text out loud before a crowd," he clarified, emphasizing the strange parallelism. "It's a vivid, tangible way to give a face and voice to a man who's been dead for hundreds of years."

I read the short fragment with interest, surprised by the originality of its imagery and the elegance of its voice. The text, in my opinion, seemed to lack the coldness typical of poor translations. Yet I also knew that no matter how I read and reread it, given my limited knowledge of English, I wouldn't be able to gauge its faithfulness to the original work. I decided then that I had to show Alioscha's work to Professor González-Lage, an expert in Anglo-Saxon literature of the period, whom I'd been collaborating with on a series of summer courses at the university of El Escorial.

"Your friend is either a madman or a very excellent translator," González-Lage replied over the phone, intrigued that Alioscha knew that work by Marlowe. "Come and see me whenever you like, and we'll talk."

I didn't hesitate to take him up on his offer and went to see him at his office the very next morning, where I found him absorbed in his routine, hidden behind stacks of papers and folders on the verge of collapse, so engrossed in deciphering old Scandinavian legends that he didn't notice my presence until several seconds after I'd said hello. I suspected right away that González-Lage would feel an affinity with Alioscha. It made sense. They had similar predilections, such as their fondness for powdery scrolls or the chaos in which they tended to work, although there was something different about González-Lage, an aridity that was less cheerful and spontaneous, an ancient and rigorous dryness that lacked Alioscha's characteristic whimsy and daring.

As soon as I handed him Alioscha's excerpt, explaining who the translator was and how I knew him, González-Lage began to examine the pages eagerly, getting to his feet and adjusting his glasses for a better look, as if it were a roll of papyrus he'd discovered after decades in dusty pyramids.

His verdict couldn't have been more enthusiastic.

"Tell him to send it to me when he finishes," he said, smiling and waving the paper in excitement. "I promise to find him an editor."

That's just what I did. I flew to Paris that very week, eager to offer Alioscha an encouraging message, happy that finally, after so many years of self-imposed exclusion and fruitless sacrifice, someone had turned up who recognized his talent. Thrilled about my friend's prospects, during the flight I developed a line of argument that would encourage him to give more consideration to the translation profession and even decided to take him to a nice restaurant, to show him that literature didn't have to depend solely on one's penchant for suffering. My aspirations vanished, however, the moment Alioscha answered the door, not because he rejected González-Lage's offer outright, but because I found him so distant and crushed by life that I knew he couldn't care less about the fate of a translation he'd undertaken practically by chance. His appearance was lamentable. His untidy beard had gone several days without a trim and there were pronounced dark circles under his eyes. His fingernails were longer and his hair greasier than I'd ever seen it. He looked, in fact, like he'd just been released from a police holding cell. It was obvious that he hadn't heeded his cousin's advice. His apartment had returned to the condition Valls had described: overturned chairs and loose tiles, an array of broken light bulbs, and a leaking ceiling in the hallway, where he'd set a plastic bucket about to overflow. The house smelled strongly of rot throughout.

"Take a seat," he said pointing to an armchair in the living room, impatient to read to me from his novel. "It's just three pages."

His excitement was palpable. Nonplussed by the impromptu nature of my visit and not even giving me time to sit down, Alioscha began to read excerpts from his book, asking me to listen for any dissonance or excessive repetition, though I was well aware that offering suggestions was as futile as recommending that he combine writing with a conventional job. So I let him recite as many pages as he pleased, unable to comprehend them, resigned that I would die before I'd manage to unravel his coded language, until, several minutes later, his three pages of text ran out and I was able to convey Professor González-Lage's praise.

Alioscha listened impassively, his eyes on the scene outside the window, so absorbed in his own thoughts that he seemed to be reveling in a midday twilight intended for him alone. Not only did he shrug at the fact that González-Lage could find him a publisher, but he also revealed something very unexpected, gesturing first at his desk, cluttered with scribbled notebooks and hundreds of loose sheets of paper, then turning back to me with a laugh.

"You want the whole book? There it is," he said, dismissing his translation hobby. "But it's practically an insult compared to the original."

Rummaging through the mess on his desk, Alioscha showed me fragments of his translation of *Henry VIII*, parts of it written on coffee-stained papers and others scrawled on a napkin, as if he'd done the work in spontaneous bursts whenever he'd felt the urge. I observed him with interest, shocked that the entire text was scattered over so many loose pages, though I confess I was more interested in seeing how Alioscha was coping with the poverty his father had imposed on him, something I could only assess when we left his apartment and I could finally observe his newfound survival techniques.

It only took a few hours to confirm that Alioscha wasn't exactly suffering in his new state of poverty. Among other things, he proved that he had different ways of procuring food, such as strolling through a nearby market, where he stole pears and apples and later showed me a few tinned goods stashed inside his jacket, or entering a patisserie where the manager offered him day-old pastries just to get him to go away and not bother the customers. He also smoked his cigarettes down to a burning nub and collected empty bottles he found on the streets, for which he reportedly received a few coins from a shop in his neighborhood. He found none of these habits demoralizing, however, for Alioscha was comfortable kneeling on the ground or accepting scraps of charity, as if those practices were degrading for everybody but him. He accepted a life of scarcity with apparent indifference, docile and calm, no signs of shame or capitulation—proud, even, of the scavenging skills with which he managed to sustain himself without depleting his savings. But though he didn't appear to suffer, many of his behaviors saddened me indeed, such as when we came to a large, landscaped square just before lunch and Alioscha made suddenly for they public restroom, where he proceeded to wash, a behavior so coarse and unusual for him that I only understood once we were back outside and he told me he hadn't been able to bathe since his water heater broke the week before. He was immune to poverty, perhaps, and indifferent to the early orphanhood his father tried to impose, but his ill-fated stay at his cousin's house in Barcelona had also dealt him other kinds of blows, such as a greater awareness of his exile, or a more mournful recognition of his existence, as if the deep abandonment he'd suffered for years wounded him now more than ever.

That sense of loneliness seemed to grip him at precisely seven o'clock that evening, when, noticing the time, Alioscha forced me to hurry back through streets and down avenues until we arrived at the Bastille, which had been our starting point. Once there, with no other explanation, he led me underground into the maze of metro tunnels. It was an irrepressible impulse that I only understood after we had been below Parisian asphalt for some time. At first, it was all very confusing and mysterious. We initially chose the line that departed from the square and crossed under the Seine, then continued diagonally through the popular Latin Quarter. However, as soon as we'd crossed that boundary, he wanted to get right off the train again and changed to one a line that returned to the bank we'd just come from, reversing our course. As he did this, he looked carefully at all the women around us, absorbed in such close examination that he seemed to forget I was with him. This is how our unpredictable roving through the maze of corridors and ghostly trains extending through the depths of Paris began. Ignoring my questions and barely speaking to me, Alioscha was immersed in a desperate search, switching lines at improbable stations, ignoring connections and more direct routes, less concerned with the speed of our progress than with following a strange route known only to him. He walked straight down the middle of the corridors, not caring if he pushed past or annoyed anyone, fixated on the legs or shoulders of one passenger or another, vigilant for any discovery, even breaking into a run when he spotted a woman with blonde hair, red shoes, and black stockings at the top of a set of stairs. Inside the cars, he scrutinized each passenger one by one, and when he was sure the elusive specter he was seeking wasn't present, he exited the compartment and repeated the same operation in the next car. Then he would abandon the line and hop on another as soon as we reached a station where, judging by his expression, he apparently recognized the signs indicating a junction.

We played that game for a long while, until nearly nine o'clock. Alioscha hot on the trail of a woman who had vanished into the city's depths, and I embarrassed by the undisguised manner by which he conducted his search. In that conspicuous way, we finally came to a remote station with graffitied walls, where Alioscha let out a long sigh and asked me to follow him outside. We were on the outskirts of Paris, one of those banlieues with uniformly tall buildings constructed out of cheap materials, a place where a light breeze barely stirred the litter on the ground, as if there was no life there apart from the noise of the cars that came and went out of simple inertia. I realized then that this was where he came evening after evening, in search of some kind of warmth, some strange and desperate peace, some vague flicker that would save him from the bleakness of his routine. Alioscha openly confessed everything to me, his gaze lost on the sight of the vulgar buildings, the brick walls between which he strived to find some short-lived, luminous fissure. "She was wearing a skirt and a blue blouse, and a white scarf around her neck—what everybody in her office must wear," he said of the woman he had seen for the first—and only—time just two weeks before. "She switched from train to train instead of taking a direct route home, prolonging her trip for as long as possible, following an itinerary she knew by heart, as if she sought refuge in the detour, stalling before she had to open her apartment door."

That strange woman had become his new obsession, the locus of all his desires, because no matter how stubborn he'd always been, Alioscha never could bear loneliness without some hope for the future. Perhaps that was for the best: that he should live clinging to the illusion that someone, soon, would find him the vast desert at long last. Regardless of whether or not he knew just how forsaken he was, the days I was with him—in addition to stocking his pantry and reminding him about Valls's cleaning tips—I joined him every afternoon on his peculiar journey through the Paris underground in pursuit of a shadow. The search began at a set time, seven o'clock sharp, the worst time to step into one of those carriages, crowded with men and women returning home exhausted after long days at work. It was not a pleasant trip. It usually took us about an hour and a half to complete, submerged the whole time in those tunnels filled with cables and metal doors, poorly lit by a few sickly lights, forced to change trains at the same stations as on our first expedition, wearing ourselves out with foolish sprints down flights of stairs and through hallways. My friend's behavior was so strange that he sometimes looked like a ticket inspector, or a plainclothes cop on duty, although due to his manifest nervousness, his behavior could be interpreted as that of a hitman. The whole campaign was waged in a state of complete absorption. He never warned me when we were about to reach one of his chosen junctions, nor when, confusing fantasy with reality, he went after a woman who had the air of his imaginary quarry, and several occasions I came close to losing him among the swaying crowd. However, no matter how hard he tried to keep everything under control, we always ended up emerging—alone and with no new clues—among those same ashen buildings where the first attempt had ended. Confronted with another failure, Alioscha glanced around despondently, his eyes reminding me of extinguished embers, and gave in to the fact that we would have to return by taxi.

Thus, though he was writing more frequently and with more passion than ever and was convinced he was working on a momentous book, Alioscha was also lonelier and more desperate. The day I left for Madrid, I sensed that he was fading into a denser fog than usual, more distant and wilted than ever, as if he knew he was destined for a feat that would devour him, a definitive self-sacrifice, doomed to defend some sort of trench where he would be the last fighter left. "I'm sure I'll find her when I make a few tweaks to the original route," he said to me as we parted. "The important thing is to have patience, and not despair. Besides, I'm already used to sleeping alone and cooking for one."

But from the outside, Alioscha didn't paint such a stalwart picture. He spoke with such apathy, such frailty, that neither his cousin Carlos Valls nor I believed him, convinced that the vision of the errant woman on the metro represented his wayward mind's latest misstep. Aware of the need to support him, in our conversations during that time I reminded him by letter and phone call that all creators suffered similar ups and downs, and that every one of the sacrifices he'd made over the years would soon be rewarded with triumph. He remained, however, indifferent to such ordinary encouragement, just as disheartened as when we'd said last goodbye, so apathetic that he barely mustered a reply to the questions he did deign to answer, capable of hanging up without warning, or sitting on the other end of the line for minutes without speaking. Yet as the weeks passed, both Valls and I began to notice hints of new emotion in his voice. It was a slow recovery. His voice was more resolute, livelier than before, and there were also other tell-tale signs, such as his incomprehensible allusions to a nursing home, his thoughts on love affairs disadvantaged by an age difference, or other baffling references to the sober architecture of the main building at the Sorbonne. But we only realized that Alioscha had indeed experienced some significant change when all communication from Paris abruptly ceased, and days and then weeks passed with no answer to our phone calls. His silence lasted almost three weeks, and we feared his end had come prematurely. Carlos Valls, aware of his cousin's tragic inclinations, was the first to react, but I was the one charged with flying to Paris so that Alioscha wouldn't be upset by the idea of his father's long shadow trailing Valls. "If I go, he'll think Bartomeu's behind it, just wanting to control him like he's a child," an alarmed Valls told me after another unsuccessful call to the apartment in Oberkampf. "It's better if you visit and make sure it's nothing more than a faulty phone."

But such reassurances wouldn't come easy. In fact, my first impression of the state of things came when I discovered my friend's apartment filled with dead plants, the air dusty and stale with the sepulchral funk of long-abandoned mansions. The initial statements I took from neighbors were not very hopeful either. "He went out just like any other day and hasn't been seen since," the supremely curious and talkative doorwoman explained as she unlocked the door to his Oberkampf apartment. "He hasn't even come for his mail." Alioscha going missing was something neither Valls nor myself had anticipated. Bewildered by this new development, alarmed by the possibility that Alioscha might have suffered an accident and was lying somewhere with a broken leg, or that he had chosen to spend the nights on a bench in one of the thousands of squares in Paris, over the following days I searched everywhere he might have gotten lost. I looked for him at all hours and in all places, the cafés and parks he used to frequent and the metro tunnels we'd roamed together, following the elusive trail of his imaginary lover. But no matter where I searched, after four days I still didn't know if he was alive or dead or whether I should to the police, but then Carlos Valls remembered a few of the last words his cousin said to him. "He babbled something about a nursing home," he explained, intrigued, on our daily phone call. "It seemed like maybe he ate or slept there sometimes or looked after the flowers in exchange for a bit of cash."

We both began to recall bits of information present in Alioscha's chatter, vague references inserted among other general remarks, brief allusions in which he obscurely mentioned an odd job whose only problem was the commute.

Connecting the dots, we were able to deduce that Alioscha might have started work at a nursing home in the Saint-Denis district.

"Once, he described a stormy Sunday when the bus ride took almost three hours," said Valls, giving me the address of the only residence home that there appeared to be in the area. "It sounded like he could have been returning to the city, exhausted from mopping floors or taking care of the elderly."

The next morning, having confirmed the address Valls had given me was correct, I headed out to Saint-Denis on an intercity bus, a slow journey of over half an hour that took me down roads and past office buildings free from any trace of Parisian monuments. During the course of my unhurried approach, I realized the absurdity of my endeavor—not only were we uncertain that Alioscha was there, at a nursing home whose name he'd never even mentioned, but we'd been led there thanks only to a couple of words he'd uttered seemingly at random.

Saint-Denis was very different from the neighborhoods Alioscha tended to frequent. In fact, as soon as I got off the bus, I realized I was in one of those well-developed areas whose very existence must have given my friend nightmares. To one side, there was a large supermarket with a parking lot out front, filled with hundreds of cars, and to the other, streets so quiet they seemed uninhabited, lined with family homes and other recently constructed buildings, all equipped with gardens and well-defined plots.

Making my mission even more absurd was the fact that it was Sunday, a day when almost nobody worked. Thus I was certain of failure, convinced I'd wasted several hours on another false lead, when I finally located the nursing home—having mistaken the address more than once—and approached the guard at the entrance. His reply took me by surprise. "Sure, he's got a job here, just on weekends," he said, opening the gate and pointing to a serene white residence set on landscaped grounds. "He might be in the physician's office now, taking somebody's temperature." Apparently those were the kinds of tasks Alioscha was assigned while at the complex—not a doctor's duties, but those of a part-time caregiver. Alioscha, I would later learn, was restricted to distributing syrups and pills and taking temperatures, with instructions to call the hospital in case of emergency.

Far from carrying out his vaguely apothecarial function, however, Alioscha immersed himself in other recreational activities, a discovery I made soon after entering the property. I walked the path that led to the residence, admiring the perfectly mown lawn and the harmonious scene of the whole place and mystified that Alioscha worked there. I'd already started up the front stairs when suddenly I heard a melody coming from the rear of the garden, a serene, old-fashioned tune that would have been popular in the 1940s. Skirting the building, I came to the part of the property shielded from the noise of cars and passing pedestrians, and in that flower-filled spot with clay paths meant for enjoying walks in the sunshine, learned why I was hearing songs from another time. I saw a tree taller and thicker than the surrounding bushes, which must have offered dense shade in summer. At its base was a wooden table, the kind used for outdoor luncheons in springtime, and on the table sat an old record player. Gathered around the dusty old contraption were about twenty elderly residents whom the excitement of the party appeared to have been rescuing from the infirmities of age.

My friend Alioscha was among the crowd, as happy and amused as any of them, deep in the joy of a celebration reminiscent of an old village fête. His uniform was the only thing to distinguish him from the others. He was dressed in a white coat and green pants, like the other nursing home employees, but he seemed to exert no authority over the residents. Instead of ensuring that no accidents occurred, I found him dancing, hands on the waist of a woman with white curly hair who must have been eighty years old. Not all the guests were enjoying the exuberance of the music the same way. Some, those who couldn't walk or were most affected by age, watched the dancing from their chairs, but just as gaily as those who moved around the tree, lightly tapping their feet or bobbing their heads in time to Alioscha's choice of song, as if the whole event were a pagan festival made possible by my friend's express approval.

So it was: Alioscha was the director of the festivities, the mastermind behind that small-scale rebellion, the one who encouraged a bit of fun outside the rules. When the record ended, he put on a new one and quickly set the needle again. But before the music began and its evocative spell transported them to the past, he called for a brief moment of silence, putting a finger to his lips, and said a few words about the merits of the singer they were about to hear. His role was to enliven the elderly. To that end, as the new melody began, he encouraged them to clap along or tap the wooden tables with their elbows. When the song seemed about to end, he lowered the volume and enjoined those feeble voices to mumble along to the chorus.

He was in an evident state of exaltation. He seemed overcome by one of his fleeting deliriums of optimism, easily forming and breaking up dancing pairs, energetically conducting the rising beats of the music with his hands. He was in constant motion, urging those who rested to get up and dance again, always energetic and passionate, bright-eyed and grinning. Seeing him so radiant, so luminous, I understood that at forty years old, Alioscha felt closer to those elderly residents with fading memories than to anybody else. It was like he hoped to travel with them down a whimsical return road to childhood, through a hazy and redeeming mist, where he could behave according to the liberal norms of fantasy rather than reality's much stricter rules.

When after a few minutes my friend finally noticed me standing just meters away, I too had to dance with the white-haired woman, whom he introduced as his favorite partner. I even helped organize a group dance where the residents were to raise their arms above their heads and wave their hands in unison. I thus found myself inevitably subject to Alioscha's fancies, obliged to spin around in the arms of ladies who needed a cane, or hum songs from my grandparents' era, unable to temper his enthusiasm until the music stopped.

He only explained himself when the party had come to an end.

"I finish work when the residents are called to dinner at nine," Alioscha said as we carried the old record player inside the building. "But I usually take advantage of my time here to go over the pages I've written during the week."

Still out of breath, invigorated after several hours of activity, Alioscha showed me an office where, on the desk, pages of his novel lay alongside bottles of aspirin and thermometers. He pointed to a roulette wheel and some game chips, claiming he also organized clandestine gambling sessions in the garden. I suspected, however, that there were other reasons for his enthusiasm besides writing and entertaining a group of octogenarians.

I was right. I learned of his new situation on our return trip to Paris. The dim light on the bus, the tinny murmur of music from the radio, the muted Sunday night air, must have seemed to Alioscha befitting of confession as we rode past the tall office buildings. Alioscha apologized for not disclosing that he had left his Oberkampf apartment for a much cheaper rental in the Belleville neighborhood. It was also then, after several extraneous remarks, that he finally confessed pleasurably that, since making the move, he had needed to work to support another person. All those changes in accommodation and activity were owed to a young student eager for adventure. Her name was Camille. "She's completely different from Élene," he insisted—a judgment that would over time prove entirely incorrect—wrapping up his euphoric tale as the bus pulled into the nearly deserted station. "An intelligent girl who would never interrupt an afternoon of writing on account of a messy house."

Alioscha spoke of her as if she were the perfect woman: optimistic and understanding, sensitive to his artistic aspirations, and capable of standing by him no matter what hardships he faced.

"I'll write my best books with her," he concluded, having recounted how he'd discovered her and convinced her to run away from her aunt's house. "It will be like she dictates the works to me, and I merely put her words on paper."

Just weeks after meeting her, that was, indeed, his idealized and utterly flawed idea of Camille, as he was still unaware that there was likely no less suitable ally for his aims in the entire city. Over the course of nine delirious months, the young Camille did nothing but attack him daily for his withdrawal and abstraction and for succumbing to his characteristic and persistent melancholy, which was akin to blaming him for having fought to the point of madness and failure to achieve his dream of being a writer. She was, after all, a very green and anxious student, overwhelmed by the mistake she'd made of running off with the wrong man. She insulted and hurt him in the most painful possible way: consistently denying him her close companionship, refusing to share a bed with him, even forcing him to sleep on a bench outside their home until that moment when, driven by incurable fevers, she gave in and called her father who whisked her away back to the family home and Alioscha was left alone and defeated, with only one thing left to do: finish *Attila* and gather the drugs he would need to kill himself.

WHETHER OR NOT it was the main reason for his breakdown, Camille's departure marked an irreversible cataclysm, a definitive blow for Alioscha, who from then on slipped into such a precipitous decline that at times it seemed he wanted to announce his death before actually dying. It is true that the young woman's departure brought about some positive effects, since it ended nine months of agony in torturous cohabitation, freeing him from daily shouts and scorn, insults and arguments. Yet the emptiness of his basement apartment, where he lived without any contact with the outside world, left Alioscha as if stranded on a kind of timeless beach, a hallucinatory landscape. As if instead of residing in an impoverished Paris suburb, he was crawling along high, steep cliffs above a sea of lunar waters, so detached from reality that it seemed like, rather than succumbing to the drugs' poison, he might gradually dissolve into a boundless mist.

Regardless of the manner of his eventual death, everything I discovered on my trip following his call for help confirmed just how hard and unfair life had always been for him. His passion for writing—the courage and perseverance with which he defended it, the purity of the dreams he'd sketched in his youth, during his early illumination—caused him to suffer all kinds of punishment, a victim of his own ambitions until the day he died. Indeed, by that point, ten years after he'd arrived in Paris, to the rest of the inhabitants of his neighborhood Alioscha was already an odd character, one of the many ruined men wandering its streets like the wasted old evangelical predicting biblical plagues from a cardboard box or the drunk reminiscing about his aristocratic lineage from the bench where he sleeps. But the disastrous February of my visit, in addition to the collective scorn and routine mockery of Alioscha's door-to-door garbage collection, he also suffered a much more dire affliction: he was obsessed by his work to an extreme degree and became increasingly unable to manage to put on clean clothes or to distinguish tangible reality from the most deceptive of fictions.

That was the state of affairs when I landed back in Madrid and contacted Valls immediately. I was sure that if we didn't keep a close eye on him, he would end up wasting away, forgetting, even, to feed himself. As expected, his cousin shared my concern. He too was worried about Alioscha taking care of himself after Camille's departure, since—despite treating him almost violently—she had at least prevented him from completely neglecting himself in certain material respects.

"If he came home with muddy shoes, if he wanted to skip a meal and keep working, if he refused to go to bed and stayed up to finish a book, she straightened him out," Valls continued. "If we don't go and see him frequently, he might never leave his desk, even if the building crumbles around him."

That's exactly what we did, of course, until the day of his death in November. For when he'd finished his book, when he'd written the last word of the last sentence, Alioscha seemed to suffer an incurable vertigo, terrified by the prospect of his self-imposed exile without the solace of work. His cousin and I, aware of his anguish and helpless witnesses to his quest, did everything in our power to save him, although neither of us could offer him the one thing he truly needed: some form of permanent companionship, without the interruptions of trips back and forth or a hotel's impersonal chill. All our efforts proved futile. During that time, Valls—who predicted Alioscha's end long before it occurred—flew to Paris at least once a month. He returned from each visit with more foreboding, saddened after accompanying Alioscha to his appointment with the goldfish in the pond or taking him to a barber to get a proper haircut. My prognosis was no more optimistic: I always found him the same, anxious and confused, talking to himself on the streets and forgetting what he was saying mid-conversation, as if he were trapped in a glass jar, bouncing off its walls, terrified by the ugliness of his reflection. Meanwhile, Alioscha, whether conscious of his downward turn or not, worked all day on *Attila*'s convoluted pages, its chaotic and dark paragraphs, as tangled as his own feverish ramblings. As he wrote without rest, submerged in a never-ending spasm, engaged in a long, cathartic crusade, he dismissed the positive opinions of Professor González-Lage, whose proposal to publish his translation of *Henry VIII* mattered little to him. "He said he didn't want to waste time rifling through his papers," González-Lage informed me at one of our meetings at the Complutense. "And that if I thought translation was so good, I could go to Paris and dig through his desk myself."

In truth, Alioscha demonstrated no enthusiasm whatsoever at the idea of the publication of his translation of the famous Elizabethan playwright. Nor about other more concrete incentives, like the short review I gave him in *El Paseante* around that same time. He showed complete indifference after reading it, as if he no longer cared about anything—neither recognition nor fame—exclusively engrossed in a perpetual written babbling, like a sorcerer muttering spells. He even spurned a Paris visit from his cousin, who brought along the publisher of Alioscha's first and only novel, *Vital Ventura Saeculi*, and refused to adjust his work schedule to accommodate one of the few men who had bet on his work. "We had to twist his arm to get him to agree to a coffee in his basement apartment—and then it was so cold we couldn't even take our coats off," Valls told me, conveying the editor's alarm. "At one point we were talking about other authors in his generation, and Alioscha just got up and went to his desk without a word. He sat there writing in a notebook for a few minutes, totally unfazed by the fact that he had a guest, and certainly not taking advantage of opportunity that man's presence represented."

In reality, my friend was the same as ever, immune to temptation, his attention floating in the nebulous distance, and just as imbalanced in his expression of his passions—more outbursts of violence as well as greater inclinations toward tenderness. In April, shortly after Alioscha's ill-fated meeting with his publisher, Bartomeu insisted on accompanying Carlos Valls to Paris. At one point, Alioscha grabbed his father by the lapels, shaking him and shouting, ready to hit him for saying that he was still as much of a coward as when, as a child, he used to hide under the bed during thunderstorms. Yet minutes later, with Bartomeu gone, Alioscha dug through a shoebox from the back of a closet and handed Valls some seashells from the Brittany coast, which he said he bought at the market with Valls's children in mind, regretful that he hadn't had more time to teach them about the mysteries of the sea. "Then he remembered a summer long ago, one August that we spent together in a small village in Girona, when we built a wooden raft from loose planks and decorated it with a black pirate flag," Valls told me upon his return to Spain, describing the nostalgia that had suddenly gripped Alioscha, who seemed to refer to Valls and his children as if he were saying goodbye to them forever. "And then, as I was leaving, he did something unexpected: he thanked me for my trips to Paris, hugged me tightly, and told me that without my support, he would have been like a blind man casting about for the exit, while everybody around him laughed."

Tragic, introspective, infinitely tender, as credulous and sensitive as always, that was Alioscha in June 1990, five months before he took his own life, when, eager to meet and speak with him, Professor González-Lage proposed that we invite him to the university campus at El Escorial.

He mentioned the possibility when we were attempting to organize the summer courses amid the chaos of his office, stepping away from his desk and pacing anxiously around the room, giddy with what he found an irresistible idea.

"He could participate in a few lectures, like plenty of other writers who give talks," González-Lage continued, already imagining Alioscha speaking before a packed auditorium. "The 'Censorship and Literature' lectures, for instance, comparing the obstacles facing writers in 1950s Spain with what authors suffered in Shakespeare's age."

We both knew the pretext was a flimsy one, an easy and opportune excuse, and one of the many attempts we made over those months to save him from his ordeal.

Carlos Valls knew it too, and from the outset, he was a proponent of the view that there was no better palliative against Alioscha's gloom than getting him out of his Parisian lair for a few days. "Yes," Valls said with sad irony, encouraging me to extend the invitation. "If he doesn't leave his hole in the basement more often, he might wake up one day and find he's been turned into a fossil, head fused permanently to the table, like a desiccated plant."

I traveled to Paris alone, on a mission, convinced of how beneficial the clean air of Madrid's mountains would be for Alioscha. He had rambled on during our last conversation, calling me Quixote, one of the characters in his book, instead of my own name. Given that I'd feared I would find him completely sequestered, drowning in his own madness, I was surprised to see that, instead of having to search for him among the wreckage of his basement as I had on other occasions, I found him waiting for me in the hotel lobby, eyeing the clock on the wall like he'd been there for hours in anticipation, so we that might enjoy the early May sunshine together. He was so exalted when he saw me step out of the taxi and head toward reception that he leapt from the sofa and called to me loudly, holding his camera aloft and claiming that there was no light more suitable for his photographs than the one that shone that very morning.

Such was Alioscha's urgency to get outside that he barely let me bring my bags to my room, drawn by the radiant sun shining on parked cars and marble monuments.

"We could lose this light any minute," he said, agitated, pointing to the Parisian sky, explaining that we needed to leave immediately for Saint-Denis. "Either you seize the opportunity, or it's whisked away forever by a passing cloud."

It was all he seemed to care about: finally enjoying the clean, potent rays after the lingering fog of winter. Oblivious to my questions, he declined to clarify whether his decision to rush to Saint-Denis obeyed some artistic rationale, and instead we boarded the usual bus that left Paris, past tall buildings and concrete bridges, and stopped in the suburbs, very close to the nursing home, as if it were a Sunday and he had to work.

But when we stepped off the bus, Alioscha set off in the opposite direction from the home, down a quiet, tree-lined residential street with large mansions and walled gardens on either side, one of the thoroughfares for wealthy families where all was silence and expanses of green. Alioscha, indifferent to that peace, impervious to that tranquility, ignorant of the contrast between his leper's prison and those comfortable homes, moved quickly and assuredly, eyes straight ahead, pulled steadily toward a mysterious destination.

We walked in silence for several more minutes, he leading the way and me trailing behind, engaged in a cryptic, unintelligible pursuit. Before I could ask for an explanation, Alioscha abruptly smiled and stopped before a huge mansion, one of the area's most modern and luxurious, with flowers and vines and an elegant façade, and a vast garden protected from the sidewalk by a wall over two meters high.

Neither the gleaming opacity of the mansion's windows nor the dogs barking behind the gates seemed to dissuade Alioscha from his unspoken plan.

"Stand there," he said, pointing to the trunk of a chestnut tree growing beside the wall. "I'll go up first, then you."

Having confirmed that we weren't being watched, I made a step with my hands, per Alioscha's instructions, and helped him clamber up onto the tree. Once safely perched on a thick branch, he pulled me up behind him. The chestnut tree was tall and leafy, its foliage so dense that our indistinct, barely human shapes were barely visible from the street, but my friend moved through its extensive architecture of sprawling branches with the agility of an expert climber. Yet instead of going in for feats of balance, Alioscha made a beeline for one side of the tree, a lateral branch that grew out toward the building, where he settled into a prone position, motionless on his belly, camera ready in his hands, as focused as a sniper patiently waiting for his target. We held that ridiculous position for almost half an hour, roosting, still and silent, Alioscha's eyes fixed on the front door and me lying behind him, clutching at his ankles, entirely unsure what we were doing there. I had just about surrendered to the thought that I was trapped in another of his delirious mirages when suddenly a young woman emerged from inside, alone, bored, walking listlessly. What we had been waiting for. I immediately noted the age difference between them, for she couldn't have been more than twenty, and was strikingly beautiful: blonde, tall, and very thin, wearing frayed jeans and a faded T-shirt with cut-off sleeves—shabby clothes she probably only wore around the house.

Her appearance stirred my friend, who inched his way further down the branch, angling for a better view, while she lingered by the wicker tables and chairs on the verandah. After a few moments of indecision, as if hesitating whether to go back inside or stay where she was, the girl began to drift idly through the garden, with no purpose but to let time pass. Observing the miracle of her body illuminated by the light, Alioscha began to photograph her, getting in as many shots as possible: the girl reclining on a lounger by the pool, distractedly fidgeting with the rake, picking up the watering hose.

He was so deeply engrossed that he made no reaction when, almost tumbling to the ground, I grabbed hold of his belt, nor when a confused pigeon mistook him for a section of tree and alighted briefly on his back. The girl was the sole object of his interest. Ignoring the risk of breaking branches, for as long as she was in his view, he took photo after photo, never lowering the camera from his face. He acted like he was witnessing some unrepeatable spectacle, loathe to miss a single flash of her figure, as meticulous in his work as an impressionist painter determined to capture the twilight in a Far Eastern port.

The girl was his secret, the reason we were both hiding like thieves in the branches of a chestnut tree as the warm spring breeze grew stronger. And that wasn't his first or last morning in pursuit of her, either, as I was to discover. All of his activities revolved around the young woman who fought boredom in her high-walled Eden. The moment Alioscha saw the sun was shining, and assuming the girl would favor being outside in the fresh air, my friend rushed us to the bus to Saint-Denis, forgetting the secondhand bookstores along the Seine and the architectural beauty of the buildings in the center of Paris. Once in position at the heart of that luxurious street, he would station himself at his lookout post and wait patiently for the young woman to leave the mansion, hungry to photograph her again. Sometimes he was even lucky enough to catch her while she was still inside, thanks to a window that offered him the thrilling vision of his muse applying makeup or reading on her bed.

His admiration clearly went well beyond bounds of normalcy. More proof of his madness was that, in addition to capturing her image under such abnormal conditions, camouflaged as if engaged in a military operation, once back in his basement rooms, he arranged the pictures throughout the entire space, even lighting candles in front of each picture as if they were religious shrines. When night fell and the lights were turned off, his basement quarters took on the eerie and sacred glow of a medieval chapel.

Yet his fixation on the unknown young woman in no way implied that he was neglecting his novel. On the contrary, as he continued to expand his photographic archive with portraits of his new muse, Alioscha wrote with more fervor than ever and showed no signs of fatigue, although he was just as slow and meticulous, able to spend an entire day reworking what he'd written the day before. During that time, when he was so close to his death and so close to finishing the final passages of his book, he took to memorizing whole pages, even complete chapters, and reciting them aloud on the streets or in restaurants, straining to hear any dissonance previously undetected in the echo chamber of his basement. Yet no matter how fervently Alioscha threw himself into his work or how many peculiar techniques he applied to his writing, the text suffered and would continue to suffer from an irremediable flaw: the language was impenetrable. Not because he employed an arcane dialect of Spanish, or any other foreign language, but because it was the language of a man possessed, comprehensible only to those suffering the same affliction.

His obsession with writing, the unbreakable witching-hour rapture into which he plunged at his desk, had already caused noticeable deterioration in Alioscha. For one, he ate little and poorly, more out of habit than to meet his body's needs, and lived a completely sedentary life, except when he went to Saint-Denis and climbed the chestnut tree to admire the unintentional poses of his surveilled subject. His appearance—pale, with dark circles under his eyes, rumpled hair, dressed in clothes that grew more tattered by the day, already steeped in the neglect many older men succumb to after losing a spouse—caused people look at him sideways out in public. Broadly speaking, this decline led to a cooling in his interactions with those who had regular contact with him, but now either withheld their greetings or took cheap shots at him on the street, signs of scorn that Alioscha now apparently regarded as ordinary gestures.

The ordeal of collecting his neighbors' garbage remained the most egregious of the routine affronts, with various onlookers keen to throw fruit peels or douse him with a bucket of water. Sometimes neighbors hid their garbage under cars, forcing him to crouch down and drag the bags out before the trucks arrived. These torments got increasingly macabre, like the night Alioscha discovered that one of the sacks he carried was dripping blood and, horrified, opened it to find a dozen dead pigeons. Despite everything, he coolly accepted these insults, as if his reality wasn't one of shoving and laughter at his door, but another, more fantastical and ethereal existence: that of writing his impenetrable novel and safekeeping the stolen images of his muse.

I spent my brief stay entirely at Alioscha's beck and call, wholly devoted to his whims. Only on my last night, when we'd returned from Saint-Denis and my friend was reveling in the enthralling images he'd managed to catch of the bored young woman stubbornly skimming fallen leaves from the pool, did I find the right moment to invite him to the summer lectures.

"Okay," he remarked simply, as if what he wanted was for me to stop talking, his eyes open to the electric night of the city. "We'll go to your professor friend's conference."

But in the weeks that followed, Alioscha ignored all preparations for the lectures, forgetting, perhaps, the promise he'd made, or simply absorbed in one of his creative raptures. If not for my persistence, he wouldn't have made it to El Escorial at all. But I hounded him daily, and emphatically so, and when the time came, he couldn't back out, caught as he was in a dense web of flight reservations and departure schedules that he couldn't escape.

"I'll try to make the plane on Monday," he said, somewhat offhandedly, as if it bemused him to see me suffer from the uncertainty. "Although I couldn't get past airport security the last time I tried to go to Madrid—I didn't have my passport."

Despite his past issues with documentation, Alioscha arrived in El Escorial as expected, at precisely five in the afternoon, bringing all his light and madness with him. He immediately greeted me with quotes from the *Odyssey* in classical Greek, explaining that his new goal was to learn several dead languages in order to read certain texts in their original voice. Then we checked him into the guest accommodations, a small hotel with the air of a mountain inn, situated right across from the austere and rigorous Herrerian-style basilica with views of the flat plains in the valley ripe for a blanket of mist.

Initially, everything seemed to suit him just fine. On the first and second days, he mingled with the other speakers, sharing meals and conversation just like everyone else. He got caught up in unproductive debates about the work of several pre-war Spanish poets and at times seemed so participative that he seemed well-versed with similar gatherings. He even exchanged addresses with a couple of professors, a sign of how comfortable he felt, delighted to meet one of González-Lage's colleagues who was an expert in surrealist poets, or to chat with an Italian professor who interpreted Homeric hymns in a manner as unique as Alioscha's own. Yet however he tried to mimic the others' ways, Alioscha could not go unnoticed; he couldn't hide his many peculiarities—like his obsession with stepping on the tiles in a specific order—nor could he suppress the excesses of his imagination. In one such instance, during an official tour of the monastery gardens, as the group proceeded under a vine-covered arched trellis, Alioscha, in a fit of playfulness, overcome by an irrepressible urge, gave the others the slip in order to lose himself among the spiral-shaped shrubbery, laughing as he recalled the metaphysical significance several Latin American writers attributed to the symbol of the labyrinth.

"Trapped. For eternity!" he exclaimed from his crouched position behind the bushes, much to everyone's astonishment. "Here you will watch me die of hunger and thirst, cloistered above the valley, like a desert paradise."

Alioscha's singular nature—untamed and anarchic, allergic to clichés and timid modes of thinking—was most evident in his late-night conversations. After nightfall, when the streetlights around the hotel came on, he would sit on lobby couches with the other guests. During those conversations, he sometimes expressed himself with an unusual vehemence, even violence, dominated by some brilliant idea, armed with a conviction that obliterated any potential disagreement. But other nights, if the topic of conversation didn't interest him or he grew bored with the cold technicalities with which some literary work was being dissected, he would either sit for hours in silence or abruptly get up from his seat and unapologetically leave the room.

His absences usually coincided with the moment the gatherings lost intensity and the air grew thick, as the academics discoursed on their respective publications and research methods. Such conditions disappointed Alioscha, who became suspicious that everyone around him was trying to bottle up their favorite poets' lines in little vials. "I hear them and feel betrayed," he said on Tuesday night, as he escaped the smoke and coffee-filled room, irritated by the way a critic picked apart the novels that had captivated him in his youth. "As if the solid sandcastle we'd been building together was suddenly toppled by the wind."

His displeasure with the conversations steeped in cold, scientific formality also reared its head at midday on Wednesday, just before he was due to present, when Professor González-Lage, after reading the lecture that Alioscha planned to give alongside the other speakers, asked him to include a few bibliographic citations.

"At least when you send the article to me for publication," he clarified, handing back the papers and making a comment about the font and indentation. "We publish the presentations later in a journal distributed to major universities."

On understanding that his commitment went beyond a simple presentation and his work would instead require rounds of corrections, Alioscha looked at the professor in shock and slowly put away the papers. Then, still without a single complaint or question, he shuffled down the hallway to his room without a backward glance, a reaction we initially attributed to his anxiety about the upcoming talk. Hours later, however, we realized it was something much worse. What we couldn't imagine as we watched him walk away past the walls hung with engravings of the monastery was that this small bureaucratic hurdle in the publication process would so discourage him.

Indeed, although we'd reminded him more than once that his colloquium was scheduled for six o'clock, when the time came, Alioscha did not appear in the lecture hall. After waiting a few minutes and verifying that he hadn't gone to another room by mistake, González-Lage decided the event would have to start anyway, and I went off to look for him. As I searched, I was by turns amused by my friend's latest antics, fascinated by his knack for escape, and uneasy with one dark thought, the fear that he might have found some ravine in the nearby mountains favorable to putting an end to his eternal melancholic tendencies.

My search was intuitively led. With no note or message to guide me, and no clue to his whereabouts other than his habits over the course of those few days, I first went to his room, which was empty, his suitcases unpacked. Then I checked the hotel lounge and the grounds around the monastery. When I was about to return, confident that Alioscha had gone to the lecture hall on his own, I came across one of the waiters who usually served us breakfast. "Your friend, the one with the long messy hair, was walking down the road in that direction," the young man said with a snide smile, pointing the way. "He was hurrying along the shoulder, like he wanted to reach the Valley of the Fallen as quick as he could."

Only then, on hearing the waiter's words, did I think of Alioscha's epic temperament, one destined for glory and failure, with no emotion in between. He was endowed with a spirit so strong and so changeable that there could be no more fitting place for him than the Valley of the Fallen, with the silence of its mournful memories and the towering stone cross. I immediately got into the organization's car, which was parked at the entrance to the hotel, and without informing González-Lage or anyone else, drove along the winding road up to the monument, oblivious to the green slopes and charm of the landscape, forgetting all my previous searching, sure now that I would find him at that grim sepulcher which had become a mere historical attraction. The premonition was so powerful that I didn't hesitate to abandon the main road and take a detour, just six kilometers after leaving El Escorial, nor did I bother looking for his figure among the pines on the roadside. And I certainly didn't consider the possibility that it was all a ruse, that Alioscha might have bribed the hotel employee into giving me a false lead.

I wasn't wrong. When I reached the vast esplanade spread at the base of the sanctuary, I saw him standing in one of those liminal places he so loved: on the edge of that sun-scorched cement plain, opposite the basilica carved into the rock, silhouetted against the backdrop of the small, sheltered valley that looked like a Swiss mirage in the middle of the Madrid countryside.

On the outside, his demeanor was not unlike that of the other tourists: his hands were clasped behind his back and his shoulders relaxed under a gentle weight, though I imagined his inner thoughts must have been very different. I observed him a bit longer before making my approach. Captivated by the grandiosity of the monument, Alioscha seemed to be lost in contemplation of the sanctuary's porticos, absorbed in its triumphal aesthetic, the colonnades with their imperial air. After a few moments, he looked away from that disquieting architecture and turned to admire the vast horizon, as if already bored with all the eagle crests and unsettling ignominy.

There was something almost listless, apathetic, in the way he moved, in the expression of his figure, the way he lowered his chin or put his hands in his pockets and took them back out, like the weary foreign tourists who were more concerned with enjoying the mountain air than with exploring the inside of the basilica. He stood in that same position, enjoying the views from the vast balcony, as if the sunlight calmed him. When he turned to his left to look at the façade again, he noticed me walking toward him across the gray paving stones, my steps as slow and careful as if I were walking to a duel.

Our eyes met directly, unsurprised, as I slowly approached from across that granite plain dotted with scarcely a dozen people. For a moment, everything was suspended in calm. It was a pleasant afternoon, with mild temperatures and a perfectly blue sky still without summer's wretched heat, and thanks to the remoteness of that hushed valley and the purity of its breezes, there was an unusual air of peace, a sensation rather alien to the funerary complex.

But no matter how carefully I'd studied him from a distance, only when I was a few meters away, close enough to notice his untied shoes and his usual white shirt stained with coffee, did I detect a new kind of smile on his face, both sad and lucid, the result I felt sure, of his repeated experience of disappointment. I thought he was probably deep in one of his clairvoyant raptures in which he imagined we were all mad except him.

"It looks bigger from a distance than up close," he said, pointing to the cross, as if disheartened following a bitter discovery. "You come slowly up the road, and when you actually get here, you think that, in the meantime, they've replaced the real one with a kinder, smaller version."

His voice was deeply weary, a voice so devoid of passion that it seemed permanently infused with defeat; he was, perhaps, already convinced that even if he moved to a different city or went into exile, he would never find a suitable place for himself. He looked like an evangelist preacher who had failed in his mission and now had to live out his days in desert caves.

I stood beside him and looked out with him over the hills.

There was a brief silence. Then Alioscha, as if still pondering the deceptive dimensions of the cross, picked up a round stone with bright flecks that lay at his feet. He weighed it carefully in his hand for a few seconds, then chucked it forcefully into the void.

And instead of screaming out all his accumulated frustration, he let out a gentle sigh:

"I'm going back to France tomorrow," he said, and there was no sorrow, no hint of grievance, no trace of vacillation. It was a stoicism that alarmed me. "I'll go back and finish the last pages of *Attila*, while my father calls me up to remind me that I'm nothing but a pathetic caricature of Verlaine or Rimbaud."

WITH A TEMPERAMENT prone to epic feats of literary heroism and the predilections of a Romantic born in the wrong century, Alioscha caused disconcertion in all who knew him: no one understood why he wouldn't renounce his exile, what strange reasons compelled him to persevere with his haunted writing, or what drove him to embrace such a difficult fate. Plenty of circumstances warranted these questions. He came from a wealthy bourgeois Catalan family, cultured and well-connected, which provided him with an excellent education and the opportunity to pursue numerous careers, all of which would have made it easy for him to lead a comfortable and pleasant existence. A life, ultimately, similar to that of his cousin Carlos Valls: no crises or major upheavals, rooted in a good profession, where his artistic inclinations would be limited to his spare time and would cease to be a degrading problem and become instead a prestigious embellishment.

But it was also true that, had he fallen into that comfortable trap, Alioscha would have been bereft of his peculiar mythical aura. Yes, if he had capitulated, if he hadn't been consumed by his Parisian venture, if he had resigned himself with the same resignation to which the rest of us resigned, he would have been a man cheapened by calculation and fear, drained of his inherent dignity and rare faith in literature more typical of earlier eras. My friend's unique character, a mix of the epic, the audacious, and the naive, occasioned his continual rootlessness, especially in the summer of 1990, when his break with reality proved irreparable.

This was evidenced by his final altercation with Professor González-Lage, who, despite Alioscha never having apologized for skipping out on the censorship lecture, had insisted on visiting him, convinced that nothing could be more vitalizing for a man like Alioscha than to see his translation of Marlowe published. "Maybe he isn't a creator," González-Lage said, unable to understand that Alioscha would never settle for a consolation prize. "But talent takes many shapes." The professor was not to be swayed from his attempt, not even when, having made various arguments to excuse myself from joining him, I reminded him that Alioscha had once compared the translator's practice to that of mere copyist. "Then all we have to do is make him reflect on his own statements," the professor replied, indefatigable. "Explain to him that the copyists of antiquity were the same people who did the engravings inside the pyramids."

He was so intractable that I felt I had no choice but to fly with him to Paris, both of us clinging to the desperate illusion that the exercise of translating verses from archaic English into Spanish would be a sufficient palliative for the plague that had afflicted my friend since he was practically a child.

For his part, Alioscha—whom I had to call several times before managing to get him on the phone—admitted our presence, albeit unenthusiastically, devising all the obstacles he could from the start, postponing meetings and limiting the time he spent with us. His compulsion to write, coupled with the inflexible discipline that never allowed him a full day's rest, dictated the schedule of each visit. We never enjoyed breakfast together, as we only went to his little hovel of a room sometime after noon, once he made some progress on his novel, having conjured away the anxiety he woke with in the middle of every night. The moment we stepped into his basement apartment, González-Lage undertook to help Alioscha with the translation, bringing out an old draft with specific paragraphs underlined in red and other pages marked with yellow tabs.

Their attitudes during those meetings differed greatly. While the professor, the only one of the two who spoke, was busy searching for the right term in the dictionary or pointing out a punctuation error, Alioscha ignored his advice, interrupting him in various ways. He would let plates and cutlery crash to the floor with the clatter broken dishes, or he would pretend to be asleep on the sofa. And his lack of interest wasn't just obvious in those strange editing sessions, but also present on our walks: Marlowe no longer in the picture, González-Lage behaved like the typical, good tourist he was, considerate of every church and museum, concerned only with following the itineraries in his well-worn Paris guidebook, a preoccupation exasperating to Alioscha, who rebelled against the idea that there was no pleasure to be found in simple wandering. These were, perhaps, the only occasions when I thought my friend's eccentricities might follow an intentional plan, and his sense of humor surfaced, just as irreverent and shameless as the professor was oblivious: González-Lage stopping short in a busy square to marvel enthusiastically over the façade of some neoclassical palace, for example, and Alioscha simply blew past him without slowing his pace, or when, for our edification, the professor attempted to read the inscription at the base of a statue out loud and Alioscha, perfectly aware of our companion's embarrassment, swung around a lamppost singing a popular post-war tune, like one of those Spanish emigrants who crossed the border into France in the 1950s, nothing but a bundle of clothes and a chicken under his arm.

Far from upsetting González-Lage, Alioscha's quirks led him to address my friend with even more tact, as he felt guilty that the strain of the translation had been too taxing. His sense of responsibility was such that by the end of the week, the professor had assumed the duties of an unpaid intern so that Alioscha would have no obligations other than rendering English into Spanish. Thanks to that new distribution of labor, the translation was finally finished one morning, and once the professor had carefully tucked all the pages into his briefcase, we went out to a nice restaurant. We were already discussing future fees and various publishing options when Alioscha suddenly stood and mumbled a flimsy excuse in order to step outside with the folder containing the manuscript. "I'll just be a minute," he apologized, already moving toward the exit and giving us no time to stop him. "I just want to make sure the ink doesn't disappear in the sunlight."

Before we had time to get up from the table ourselves or even fully realize that Alioscha now possessed the translation's only existing copy, González-Lage and I watched through the window in shock as Alioscha walked away slowly, calmly, down the sidewalk, eventually stopping and squatting at the curb, above a storm drain between the parked cars. He held the translation up for us to see, oblivious to the passersby who skirted around him, curious, and as he laughed and watched us euphorically, he began slipping small pieces of the text through the grates, like he was inserting plastic chips into a slot machine. He neither hesitated nor slowed his momentum, so by the time González-Lage lunged for him, all that was left in his hands were the remnants of three or four crumpled pages.

After witnessing the lunacy of the deposit made into the Parisian sewer, the professor swore off any new rescue missions.

"He's hopeless," he concluded on his way to the airport, baffled by my friend's actions. "It's like he's tied himself to the mast of a sinking ship and screams at anyone who comes close to try and free him."

But those disastrous months would include other conflicts far more painful than the sacrificed translation. The worst—because of who was involved and the accumulated rage it revealed—was his final confrontation with his father, an episode so violent that it would preclude any chance of future reconciliation. Indeed, following the altercation, Alioscha seemed effectively orphaned, even before anyone died. He and his father had had so many disputes over the years that this was the most logical end to their relationship. His cousin confided to me that it all started one day in early September when Bartomeu turned up at Valls's Barcelona apartment cursing his son more than usual, vowing to change his will to keep Alioscha from benefiting from the inheritance, humiliated by some rumor about his son's decadence that he'd just heard in his neighborhood bar. His tone, angry and defiant, showed that he'd received a blow to the one thing that mattered to him: the good reputation of the surname they shared. There was no other explanation. He was furious, banging on the table, throwing the newspaper on the floor, just like when he berated Alioscha as a child for crying at the sight of blood or for not daring to swim in the sea on account of the strong waves. He appeared unwilling, in fact, to bear the thought of being associated with a melancholic copyist who could just as well be the protagonist of a grotesque satire for even another week. It was then that Bartomeu decided he would go to Paris accompanied by Carlos Valls, who, around that same time, had published a collection of poems with a small publisher in the city.

According to Valls's testimony, once they were in the French capital, everything—from the father and son's antagonistic personalities to the first of the autumn rains—contributed the atmosphere of violence. Even the happy news of the publication of Valls's book of poems led to venomous comparisons and increased the tension between Bartomeu and my friend: "At lunch, at dinner, every time we sat down on a bench by the Seine, my uncle harped on Alioscha with the same old line," he told me by phone the morning of his return to Castelldefels. "He would tell him to be like me; not expose himself to failure and ridicule; find a respectable, well-paid job; the myth of the poor, unsung artist was in the past and all the writers he had known always wore new clothes and lived in nice neighborhoods."

That, and other, even less pleasant things, for as Valls explained, Bartomeu, perhaps still embarrassed by the malicious comments circulating in Barcelona, didn't stop at overwhelming Alioscha with advice on accepting a life structured according to the family's standards. In the days leading up to the argument that would cause a permanent rift between them, Bartomeu reproached his son endlessly and on any pretext: the crass way he held the cutlery, a tremor of his hand that caused him to spill soup on the tablecloth, the faces he made at the dogs they passed on the sidewalk, the fact that he'd nicked his cheek while shaving. But beyond those rather mundane reproofs, his cousin, with a mixture of guilt and sorrow, recounted what happened the last night of their stay: they were already back at the hotel, about to go up to their rooms to pack, when his uncle insisted on returning to Alioscha's apartment, angry because his son had turned his back on him when it was time to say goodbye. "He was so furious that he smashed an ashtray and kicked the reception table—he even shook an employee who dared request that he calm down," Valls continued, his voice hushed and secretive, as if despite being in his home in Castelldefels, he was a spy revealing a critical communication. "I couldn't stop him from going back out and hailing a taxi, which he ordered to take him to Belleville. And despite the traffic and the distance, the car had the unhappy fortune of reaching Alioscha's door during the brief window of time that he was collecting the garbage while the neighbors tripped him and called him names."

Bartomeu, who'd known nothing of that humiliation, now saw his son made into a grotesque shadow, a carnival attraction, a piece of debris among the filthiest debris of Paris. It was as if he had caught Alioscha face-down in a pile of manure. Not only did he not defend him, but he attacked his son with more hatred than anyone else. His reaction was so violent that balcony doors and windows were quickly opened to enjoy the spectacle. "He went straight to him, before the taxi had even pulled away, insulting him in a Spanish incomprehensible to the crowd, reminding him with contempt that no one in their family had ever been as insignificant as he was. Alioscha responded by dropping the garbage bags and pushing him aside, and Bartomeu retaliated with another shove, so they fought like two strangers outside a bar, falling down and getting back up in the middle of a fevered crowd," continued Valls, who assured me that he'd only been able to separate them thanks to the intervention of some city workers. "It looked almost like a boxing match, the streetlights glaring down on the fighters, the laughter, the clapping, the voices galvanized by an ancient blood lust and violence, the communal ecstasy at the sight of twisted faces and staggering bodies."

After that brawl—reminiscent of pair of young thugs scuffling outside a bar—father and son never saw each other again. Having lost the company of Élene and Camille long before, and now with no more visits from Bartomeu or Professor González-Lage, Carlos Valls and I became Alioscha's last links to the world. We were also the only ones capable of making any sense of his strange behavior. In his final months, though he worked harder and more diligently than ever, Alioscha must have felt even more alone and claustrophobic, disoriented in his word jungle, trapped on a spiral staircase narrowing with each step, yet compelled to continue. His exaggerated imagination was the clearest sign of his detachment from reality. His behavior became so eccentric, so irrational, that on occasion it almost caused a public disturbance. Driven by unpredictable whims, he would tear down movie posters and lay them like rugs on the floor of his basement apartment, or ask a bus driver to stop so he could chase after a woman, or visit the goldfish in the pond in the little square, which was always empty, not only to feed them scraps of food, but also build them tiny boat-like structures resembling floating plants from small pieces of cork.

Yet his most obsessive actions involved his spying of the young woman in the mansion in Saint-Denis. He went to photograph her almost daily, rain or shine, even though he knew she would stay indoors if the weather was inclement. He was content to capture the nape of her neck resting against the window or the fleeting shadow her figure cast on the curtains. He even spent some long nights camouflaged among the branches of the chestnut tree, waiting until dawn, clutching his camera in hopes of seizing the magical moment when his muse would wake in the middle of the night, wanting a drink of water, and he could glimpse her, veiled only by her nightgown, illuminated by the lamps whose light broke the circle of shadows. But he didn't leave everything to chance. Since he liked to admire her in her full splendor, radiant and smiling in the perfect green of the garden, he came up with wondrous surprises to provoke her delight, a series of creations that seemed to form some secret communication mechanism. I was occasionally obliged to collaborate on his tricks. Among others, one Saturday I helped him transport the old record player from the nursing home to the fence around the mansion, where we climbed to watch the young woman dazzled by the music emanating from nowhere, though perhaps she was even more amazed the day she discovered the garden decorated with tinsel and colored balls, as if someone had dreamt up Christmas in October just for her. Given his devotion to her, the number of photographs he took began to overwhelm him. He accumulated so many and was so concerned with how they were to be arranged, that the walls of his basement apartment were almost completely covered. Even the only mirror in the house was bestrewn with her image, and so the easier it was for him to see his nymph in the solitude of her garden, the harder it was to confront the face of his own sleepwalking self.

His obsession appeared to be a way of combating the self-imposed demands of writing the end of *Attila*. Indeed, many of his behaviors—which could, at times, seem like those of an already senile old man, or even a vagrant stupefied by alcohol—were evidence that, regardless of his hard work and intelligence, it would be hard for him to ever finish a comprehensible book. There were countless examples. On one of my visits, finding the door to his apartment ajar, I entered his refuge without knocking and caught him hunched over his desk, intensely focused on rearranging the same four words in the margins of a notebook full of crossed-out lines. A few weeks later, equally engrossed in his novel and eager to read me a few pages of the latest draft, he stopped on a street corner next to a large puddle, oblivious that the passing cars were splashing his pant legs.

Carlos Valls's view was no more optimistic. He described Alioscha ripping up pages in fits of frustration over some flaw in a sentence's rhythm, or abruptly getting up in the middle of a meal to return to his desk, summoned by the voices of his own imaginary creatures. "I asked him a question and he replied with a phrase from his book," he revealed, also informing me that he'd found several sheets of paper on which Alioscha had rewritten the same sentence almost a hundred times. "It's like, instead of being among us, he's already disappeared into his fictional heroes."

His end was near. I realized this in early November, on a visit where I found his apartment dimly lit by the candles burning before his favorite photographs. The faint glow gave him a somewhat priestly air, as if in that faint half-light, his hands had become shaky and his body older and thinner. Seen from the entrance, his image told me that a catastrophe had occurred. He had a black eye, like he'd been punched, and his skin was so pale it looked like it he had rubbed it away in a fit of madness, trying to rid himself of his anguish, and his left hand was covered by a cumbersome bandage.

When I closed the door and took a few steps inside, besides being surprised at the fixed way he stared at the wall, I saw him engaged in a ceremonious operation, removing the photographs one by one from the nearly bare walls and putting them into a bag, as if he were about to embark on another move.

"The bruise is the least of it," he murmured in greeting, barely nodding to acknowledge his wounded cheekbone. "More awful was seeing her run into the house, screaming in terror that someone had tried to kidnap her."

Standing in the feeble candlelight, Alioscha revealed the cause of his most recent injuries as he continued his task, collecting and throwing the photographs into the bag with the same cold, mechanical rhythm as if he were handling nuts and bolts on an assembly line. According to his account, a few days earlier he had gone to her house with the idea of hiding a parrot in the branches of the chestnut tree. He had patiently trained the bird to repeat her name, so that when she stepped outside and heard herself being called from above, she would look up to the sky, unable to locate the bird, and attribute the disembodied voice to a heavenly miracle. "Things were going as planned: I was taking pictures in a different spot from where I'd hidden the cage, well-camouflaged by the leaves. She was enthralled by the marvel, open-mouthed, eyes sparkling. Maybe she thought the sound came straight from the clouds. She moved around under the tree, searching for her invisible admirer, until she came beside the fence by the street, and I was afraid she would find me," he continued, staring at a photo he held in his hands and explaining that, as he tried to move to avoid being seen, his camera slipped, and he instinctively reached out to save it. "I lunged to one side, afraid the camera might fall on her head, and lost my balance. I came down as heavy as like a sack tossed off the back of a truck."

I could have imagined the rest of the story myself, but he didn't stop his tale, engrossed in the painful memory whose melancholy seemed to help him finish exhuming his past. The end of his courting of that mysterious Parisian trapped in her garden had been disheartening. Seeing him fall from the chestnut tree, more panicked than disappointed at unmasking her mysterious admirer, as terrified as if she had encountered a man with a knife as she stepped out of the shower, she ran to seek protection in the mansion, screaming in alarm. Alioscha, meanwhile, lay on the grass with a broken wrist, in the company of the parrot and its monotonous refrain. "I showed them where the cage was," he said as he climbed onto a chair to reach the photographs tacked high on the wall. "But even the police couldn't find it when they came. So, as they took me away, handcuffed in the car, in the confusion of sirens, cries, and the murmurs of the crowd, you could still hear the parrot's unrelenting refrain, threatening to drive the whole neighborhood mad."

Having removed those images, the last reflections of life and youth, from the walls of his basement, Alioscha insisted that we board one of the tourist-laden boats that sailed along the Seine. He looked like an errant traveler with the bag filled with photos slung over his shoulder and the apprehension of a rag-clad Irishman crossing the Atlantic a century before, forced out by hunger. Everything about our appearance suggested that we were on that boat by mistake. We obviously had nothing in common with the other passengers. We carried no maps or bags of souvenirs, nor did we lean on the side railings to observe the tall and brightly lit monuments that, seen from the river and in the company of tourists, looked like cardboard silhouettes on a 3-D postcard. We had no curiosity whatsoever about the other boats, also full of foreigners, which blew their horns when our paths crossed. Oblivious to those mock seafarer's amusements, removed from the vertigo of the immense and starry city, sick of the stale air of the living, my friend and I stationed ourselves at the rear of the boat, where we were closer to the engine's roar. The dogged wind, blowing more forcefully and freely, hit us from behind, stirred our hair and raised our coat collars, as we stood before the churning water as we left bridge after bridge behind. In that particular corner of the vessel, mostly ignored by passengers, lay a jumble of ropes, cans of paint, and an overstuffed toolbox at our feet. Our sense of isolation and intimacy deepened when, near eight o'clock, the dinner bell rang and the deck grew deserted, vacated by tourists and employees alike, no one in the corridors and all the plastic chairs empty. It felt like all the solitude and grandeur of the night were concentrated at the stern of that leisure boat, as if instead of navigating a well-channeled river, we were hanging, with bated breath, over the edge of a waterfall. But despite the sense of expectation, there was nothing but silence. We remained that way for a few more minutes, side by side and in silence, watching the wake formed by the boat's steady course as the northerly breezes grew increasingly cold and robust, violently whipping the flags and cables, until Alioscha finally broke the peace with a confession.

Coolly, calmly, his voice barely a whisper, Alioscha offered up his deepest wound, his cruelest need, the emptiness that suffocated him at night, the despair that made him confuse love with contempt and coldness with some kind of warmth. With infinite sorrow, inconsolable disappointment, he spoke, encouraged, perhaps, by the thought that the thundering engine and spirited wind might blunt the bitter directness of his words:

"I'm lonely," he said.

The barge's engines roared in time with his revelation, as if making an extraordinary effort, an unsuccessful attempt to forget, as if trying to cleanse the Seine of an indecorous stain with the whir of its propellers, and then Alioscha's declaration was followed by new silence, one graver and more defeated and possibly eternal. In the hush of the ghostly deck, a sudden gust of wind sent cigarette butts and wrappers flying and caused the boat to rise for a few moments before falling back in place, sailing on as if it had hit a bump in the road. But even rough waters couldn't sway Alioscha to move inside. He was understandably unaffected by the possibility of dying in a shipwreck, now that he'd laid bare his deepest scar. And aware that there was no point in keeping up the charade and the only thing left to do was free himself from the burden of the past, he stepped up onto the toolbox, rummaging inside the sack he carried and raising a fistful of photographs into the wind with the same heroic thrust one would hoist a torch to guide a fog-threatened ship. I put my hand on his back for fear he might lose his balance. But Alioscha held his stance for several seconds, straight and solemn, his right arm reaching toward the heavens and his left hanging by his side, as the wind ruffled his hair and shook the photographs. As we neared one of the city's most famous bridges, he opened his hand so that the secret images of the woman in the garden scattered behind us on either side of the boat, over the Seine. The heavy wind held the photographs aloft briefly before they fell into the water. The electric glow of the city was so vivid, the light from the bridge so bright, that we could clearly see the pictures descending in slow spirals, like autumn leaves, some gliding just a few meters, dizzy over the boat, and still others lifted upward by a capricious gust before plummeting as quickly as if they'd been felled by a shot.

Such was his method for purging the last memories of that Parisian girl he fell in love with from his perch in a chestnut tree. He continued to pull out photographs, desperate to lighten the load, grabbing them by the handful and letting the breeze carry them off in its invisible folds, casting them on the whims of the gale, losing them in skittering flurries of white paper that might have been the flight of doves set free. Sometimes, instead of waiting for the wind to snatch them away, he sent them flying, hucking them angrily, throwing them as far away from him as possible, so that after a clumsy flapping of hands, the boat's narrow horizon was dominated by a blizzard of small shreds of paper. He emptied the whole bag that way, in speechless ceremony, where fury and nostalgia, impotence and fatigue, mingled until nothing was left in the sack. He reached into his coat and showed me a dozen portraits. "I could only think about her," he said, as if admitting he'd been conscious of his madness, while I noted that, in the pictures he'd chosen, his model looked more beautiful than ever. Those relics, which he clutched to his chest to ward off insomnia every night, which he seemed liable to tattoo on his flesh, were to be consumed in a more spectacular fashion. With the rising sound of tourists' laughter in the background, Alioscha studied the photographs one by one, then took out his lighter and lit the corner of the first. When he saw that the fire had caught, he held it aloft toward the sky, as if cursing the heavens for the wonderful and vexing dream that life had always been for him, and after a deep sigh, released the paper and watched it waft down in a trail of sparkling embers until, with a sizzle, it was extinguished on the water. Every piece of paper, every one of those precious images, vanished like the wake of a falling star, a primitive sacrifice, illuminating with its short-lived flare the wood and metal of the boat and my friend's expressionless face, consumed in the act of offering its splendid light in the midst of shadows.

It was the last performance of his poetic spirit. The wind was so strong that the burning photographs came down slowly, several of them fluttering in the air simultaneously, creating surprising compositions in a sort of impromptu pyrotechnic display, as if we had built a bonfire only to have a sudden squall send the sparks flying.

His acknowledgment of his own despair did not end with burning photographs over the Seine. The next morning, as

I hurried to hail a taxi to the airport, Alioscha unexpectedly appeared outside the hotel. On seeing me, he smiled and hugged me, helped me with my bags and made an unexpected confession. *Attila* would be his last book. When he wrote the last word of the last sentence of the last chapter, his desire to write would be fulfilled.

"Three pages," he said, giving me a knowing look as he shut the taxi door. "Three pages and the book will be done. Three pages and I can throw my desk out the window."

That was the last time I saw him. Over the next two weeks, I spoke with him on the phone a few times, or rather, I tried to, because Alioscha would just pick up the receiver and reply either in monosyllables or with a heavy silence, breathing thickly in the emptiness of his basement apartment and ignoring my questions. Carlos Valls did make one trip to Paris during those final weeks, a short stay that led him to conclusions similar to my own when he found Alioscha immersed in activities that contained a certain funeral resonance. "One morning, when we heard on the radio that the first frosts were about to arrive, he collected several bags of stale bread for the fish in that pond," he relayed to me upon his return. "He knelt by the water and sprinkled in the crumbs, telling the fish—as if they could understand him—that soon someone else would come to break up the ice with a stick and bring them something to eat."

Valls and I knew that his delirious antics were the prelude to his ruin, the cries of a condemned man, signs from a walking ghost who leaves a smattering of clues before he hangs himself. Indeed, Valls had doubted whether or not to speak to Bartomeu about undertaking a more direct strategy to prevent the disaster that would soon come to pass. Yet neither of us chose to stop him, convinced, perhaps, that it was better for him to die in the trenches of his luminous, senseless struggle than see him reduced to a pale version of himself in an apartment in Barcelona. So delicate was that period during which our inaction made us accomplices to his suicide that, contrary to our usual habits, Carlos Valls and I barely spoke to each other on the phone, thereby avoiding the mention of something we sensed was about to happen and which we did nothing to stop. The wait was an uneasy one. A false truce, a peace forever on the verge of being broken, a kind of anticipatory grief in which we could find no relief by mourning the actual death of our friend, sunk in a dense calm, a passing fog, an uncomfortable morass in which all was disturbed by uncertainty.

So passed the early days of November, dominated by an ominous silence barely punctuated by a few unanswered calls and the continual temptation to make an unannounced visit, until one morning, when it was no longer possible to think about anything except Alioscha and his exile, a courier knocked on my apartment door. "The fastest shipping available," he said as he handed me a package and unwittingly announced my friend's date of death. "Just two days to get here from Paris."

The envelope, of course, had been sent by Alioscha. I didn't need to open it to know that inside his last words waited, his posthumous lines, the muffled, lonesome cry with which he must have agonized on the floor in his dingy room before slipping away forever: the only copy of *Attila*, the book he had fought for and was ultimately defeated by, like a fighter who spends years in the jungle, waging war for a cause he's the last to still believe in.

I opened the book to the end, anxious to read the very last page, impatient to know his last syllables among the living, his tremulous parting song, and only when confronted with those lines, which he must have typed while already in possession of the fatal drugs, could I again hear his lucent voice, the noble voice that longed for beauty and yearned to be so full and so true, the voice he stood behind with such courage and faith that it condemned him to exist in permanent state of estrangement until the day he died.

March 2013

AUTHOR'S NOTE

Alioscha, this novel's protagonist, is a character inspired by the figure of the writer Aliocha Coll, who did really exist, and some of the events referred to in this book are true: he wrote, among other things, *Vitam venturi saeculi* and *Attila*, and was a translator of Marlowe.

He studied Medicine, although he barely practiced the profession, and despite having grown up in Barcelona, he spent a good part of his life in Paris. He resided there until his death in 1990, when he finished *Attila*, which would be his final novel and was published posthumously a year later by the Spanish publisher Destino.

Other general details of this book are also real, as is the extreme complexity of Coll's works and the limited circulation they enjoyed among readers. "A kind of rather impossible literature," noted Javier Marías, who was Coll's friend and who wrote the most about him, recalling the cultured and exquisite education that characterized the real Aliocha.

The attributes and situations with which he is portrayed in this book are, however, products of the author's invention, who wanted to explore through imagination a life that was devoted to writing and which left behind a literary work so singular that it seems to be waiting still for someone to decipher it.

Certainly, Aliocha Coll's personality was different from the one reflected in this novel, and the circumstances he lived through were also different. But there is no doubt that writing occupied the central place in his life, and that he dedicated himself to it with complete audacity and honesty, regardless of the risk and sacrifice it entailed, never accepting halfway solutions that would bear him away from his creative convictions.

"Mondrian still hasn't arrived in literature," Aliocha Coll once said, expressing his desire to venture into yet-unexplored narrative territory, indifferent to the fact that such a visceral quest would bring him few rewards.

The figure of Aliocha, seldom known and with very few documents in which he is remembered, grew in this author's imagination until resulting in this much more conventional work of fiction, which may serve, perhaps, to kindle the interest Coll undoubtedly deserves.

The rest of the characters appearing in this book are entirely works of fiction, with no parallels of any kind with the people close to Aliocha Coll in life.

JAVIER SERENA

ACKNOWLEDGEMENTS

To Óscar Sipán and Mario de los Santos, who were the first to read and believe in this novel. To Fernando Marías, who was an enthusiastic and generous reader of this book and encouraged me to give it a second life.

JAVIER SERENA (Pamplona, Spain, 1982) is the author of the novels *Attila*, *Last Words on Earth*, and *Notas para una despedida*. His books have been translated into English and Italian. He has received fellowships from the Antonio Gala Foundation, the Valparaíso Foundation, the Axóuxere Foundation, and the Les Récollets residency in Paris. He is the editor of the literary magazine *Cuadernos Hispanoamericanos*.

KATIE WHITTEMORE translates from the Spanish. Her translations include novels by Sara Mesa, Javier Serena, Aroa Moreno Durán, Lara Moreno, Nuria Labari, Katixa Agirre, Jon Bilbao, Juan Gómez Bárcena, Almudena Sánchez, Aliocha Coll, and Pilar Adón. She received an NEA Translation Fellowship in 2022 for Lara Moreno's *In Case We Lose Power*, and has been a finalist for the Spain-USA Foundation Translation Prize and the Queen Sofía Spanish Institute Translation Prize, longlisted for the Dublin Literary Award, and shortlisted for the National Translation Award.